To Ida,

Charlotte K. Jammy

Inheritance
A Mixed Blessing

Inheritance
A Mixed Blessing

by

Charlotte Krepismann

Easy Break, First Time Publishing
Royal Oaks

Table of Contents

ACKNOWLEDGMENTS

Thanks to Dorothy Wall, consultant and sympathetic listener, who guided me through the book; to Carole Davis, whose writing class helped me with suggestions and encouragement; thanks to my friend and fellow writer, Hal Rauch, who suggested this title and insisted that I finally learn to use a computer. Above all, thanks to my brother, Martin Giventer, who shared my life with Mama and helped through our sad moments. My enduring love to my husband, Howard, who has encouraged me and given me his total support.

TO THE READER

It's important to understand that though all the characters are based on members of my family, so much of the plot moved into fiction for dramatic effect that the names of family members have been changed. I wrote from memory and from Mama's stories but also from the creative need to make my characters live and breathe as I saw them in my minds eye.

"The old one who is loved is winters with flowers."

(German Proverb)

Introduction

Mama died five years ago. She was the center of my life for so many years, and while I miss her, her death meant my release from worry and nagging anger. It has taken the full five years to understand what she meant to me. I feel neither pain nor sorrow. She lived a long, full life, one that was relatively happy in her old age, except for the last two years spent in a nursing home.

I hold her picture in my hand and smile back at her. All over my house are reminders of Mama: an old table she had polished to mirror brightness, a copy of Rodin's *The Kiss*, a tiny black bud vase she loved, and, in my dresser, pictures, letters, and jewelry she gave me. On my right hand, I wear the diamond ring Daddy bought for Mama for their twenty-fifth wedding anniversary. A picture of Mama and her sisters, Aunt Goldie and Aunt Nettie, stands on my bedside table and captures the past. Mama is young and lovely, with serious eyes and firm lips that show the resolution that guided her life--and mine.

It is in my head and heart, however, that I carry my memories of Mama. I remember the stories about her childhood as she told them to me, always sighing with love for the Papa who died so young. I remember how she spoke of romantic love when she met and married my own father. Love defined Mama as no other word could--love that strengthened and love that controlled. With quiet strength and stern looks that punished more than loud rebukes when I disobeyed, Mama set out the "shoulds" of my life: "You should study hard." "You should always be close to the family." And, most of all, "You should teach your children to respect you and love God." I believe I have inherited her endless ability to love and to nurture, but I fought her control until the day she died. I left the family fold and married the man I loved. I allowed my sons to make their own decisions after consulting with us. I gave Mama as much time as I could spare, but she always wanted more and more and more.

I thought I could grow up just by marrying and leaving Mama. I was wrong. Mama's love reached out to me by letters, through visits to California where I lived with my husband and children for 17 years until she followed me, and through her constant injunctions of what was "right" and what I must do to succeed. When I complained to a doctor that Mama's love was suffocating me, he answered, "Aren't you glad that you have a mother to love you?" Funny, that's exactly what Mama would have said.

Mama believed in the sanctity of the family, by which she meant her family, her six sisters and three brothers, and, of course, my grandma, whom we called Bubbie. Bubbie brought her children to this country and raised them to be close and good to each other. My brother Michael, Daddy, and I lived with the knowledge that Mama's uppermost loyalty was to the memory of her Papa who had told her that "Family was everything." Daddy suffered from jealousy all the days of his life. Michael and I made endless trips with Mama to visit her family. We were given no option. Mama created a legend for me about her Papa who could do no wrong, A man whom *I* envisioned as a Jewish Abraham Lincoln with wise and thoughtful dark eyes.

Only by breaking away from her mythic loyalty to her father could I grow up enough to separate myself from Mama. Living far away in California, I made friends as dear to me as the aunts and cousins who loved me but treated me as a child. Bringing up my own children and forging a strong relationship with my husband gave me the strength to cope with the death of one child and the mental illness of another.

I have had to split myself into many parts: to nurture my family, to devote myself to my teaching career, and finally, to find self-expression in writing--a need which I could deny no longer. I found a pathway to self-knowledge and independence, and a way to understand the old angers and jealousies, so much of which involved the profound influence of Mama.

By returning to Mama time and time again in both reality and in my writing, I realize now that she has succeeded in leaving her mark upon the world and upon me.

LEAVING PAPA BEHIND

1911   Leaving Russia

Mama left Russia in 1911 as a young girl on the edge of becoming a woman. She was sad to part with everything she knew in Horadisht but filled with dreams of a new world, with rich men and women who lived in impossibly tall buildings and spoke a strange language. Everyone in her small village worried about the unrest in the larger cities where the working people clashed with the Army and where pogroms happened almost every week. There was tension in the air every time the rabbi talked about young men leaving before the Army took them away.

Only her brother Harry was still at home. Two of her brothers had already left for America with her two older sisters, Alice and Hester, almost a year ago. Now Alice was so far away that Marsha (Mama) wondered if she would ever see her again. One night she put on the blue straw hat that Alice had bought her at the busy food market a few miles from their home. She danced around the main room that served as the children's sleeping quarters, as well as the dining room and sitting room. Then she stopped and looked at herself reflected in the big samovar that warmed the area closest to the beds. Everything she saw ballooned out to fill the round shape of the samovar: her brown eyes were like big saucers, her hat perched on her short, straight hair looked for all the world like a blue cloud come to rest on a giant's head.

Marsha dropped down onto a heavy cushion the family used for seating, put the hat in her arms, and rocked herself from side to side. She sang a song she had just made up, "If I were a bird, I'd fly to you, I'd sit on your shoulder all day long and sing of my love."

She felt a strong hand on her shoulder. It was her mother, so tall and straight, hair pulled into a no-nonsense bun, confident she could handle all problems. She wiped the tears from Marsha's face and said, "Enough with the tears. Your sister wrote to me in English, and I asked the teacher to read the letter to me. Hester and Alice have jobs in a factory sewing on blouses in Brooklyn. Imagine that. They made enough money, along with your brothers' pay to rent a house four times as big as this one. A house that is ready for all of us." Mama's eyes sparkled when she held Marsha close. Marsha could smell the clean bread aroma on her mother's apron.

She wondered how her mother could smile at the news of a new home when she had lived all her life in this little village of 300 people, all of whom lived in tiny houses so close to each other and knew everything about their neighbors.... Who could read the fastest from the Torah, which woman baked the most delicious challah on Friday, whose daughter wanted to marry whose son, who was healthy and who was sick.

Marsha looked around the room, so crowded with furniture and cooking pots, gleaming from the vigorous scrubbing her Mama gave them. Marsha and her eight brothers and sisters had slept bundled up on the three beds and sometimes ate in two shifts at the wooden table. She forgot her recent tears and asked Mama, "Will my brothers sleep in a separate room in our new house?" She was thinking of her brother Harry who coughed and coughed until he lost his breath.

"Yes, sweetheart. There will be one big room for the girls, one smaller one for the boys and a separate one for me." Marsha noticed that her mother's cheerful smile disappeared for a while. Was she thinking of Harry? What if he became very sick? Would Mama leave him here? Marsha shivered at the thought of Harry coughing his heart out every night. Surely Mama worried that Harry might have the same terrible disease that took Papa away from them.

Mama's smile returned and she reached out for Marsha's hands to swing her all around the room with a strength that never surprised Marsha. Papa had been the wise man, but Mama was like a spring breeze that moved the family on.

Every day the pile of new clothes grew as Mama worked on the old sewing machine that Papa had used in his tailoring shop. After Papa died, Mama made some money by sewing for the children of the village. Now, dressed in their new pink blouses and skirts, the girls waited outside for Mama. They laughed at Harry who paraded around like the neighbor's rooster. He was so proud of his first pair of long pants left to him by Brother Sam.

Led by Mama, the family paid a solemn visit to the mayor, who worked in the tallest building, the only one made of brick instead of wood. The mayor gave Mama all the papers they would need when they reached America. His eyes were bright with wonder--or so Marsha liked to think.

They also visited the small shul and were blessed by the rabbi. "So far away, Mrs. So many new things to see. For me, my life is here in Horadisht. May God be with you. Children," he turned to them, "remember to say your prayers, celebrate the Sabbath Queen and...." Tears spilled over onto his cheeks and found their way into his gray beard. Marsha bit her lips. It was terrible to see an old man cry.

In the days that followed, Mama kept the children busy with wrapping and packing. Only a few precious objects were to go with them to America. Not the old samovar that belonged to Papa's family. Not the old bed Mama had shared with Papa so many years. "We will take the mezuzah, of course, and the big fish pot for our first Passover in the New World. Just think, children. We will all be together again." Marsha watched as her mother stroked the copper sides of the old pot that glowed in the candlelight with a magical sheen. "I will make gefilte fish in this beautiful pot. Something old and something new." Marsha thought her mother's face glowed just like the pot she held so lovingly.

The night before they left, the house groaned and strained as all their friends crowded in with little gifts of candy and cookies for the girls and a warm sweater for Harry, who tried so hard not to cough. His mother looked at him many times that night, and a frown creased her smooth forehead.

"Harry," Marsha whispered, "don't let Mama see you looking tired and sick. Keep thinking that we will be in our big house in a few weeks. In America, you will be strong again." Her mother always said that she and Harry looked like Papa, with more delicate features and darker eyes than their brothers and sisters.

"I'll be all right," Harry answered, but his eyes were bright with fever, not the lovely glow from the candles that shone on Mama's samovar. He smiled and showed Marsha the wooden carving he had made of the samovar "I made this so we can take it with us until we can find a new one."

That night, Marsha tossed around in the shared bed, pulling the worn quilt over her cold feet and disturbing her sisters, especially Nettie, who although younger than Marsha, was very protective of Goldie and Miriam, twins who were hardly out of their baby clothes. "Ouch, Marsha! Your feet are all over my back. So stop twisting and turning already. If you're cold, take my place tonight, but tomorrow, I will tell Mama that I don't want to sleep in your bed. I'd rather sleep with the babies."

Marsha tried to settle down into the plump pillows that were filled with feathers from their neighbor's chickens. But she couldn't sleep. Harry was coughing in Mama's room and the sound filled the quiet night. Marsha slipped out of bed, feeling an immediate chill on her bare feet. The big room was dark except where the moon peeked through the clean white curtains Mama left as a gift for the next family that would live in their house. She threw a light blanket across her shoulders and put on her shoes. She knew exactly where she wanted to go.

Her breath came fast as she slipped out the door and struggled across the pebbled path in front of the house. She knew she had ten more houses to pass before the small meadow, covered with tiny flowers gray-white in the moonlight, that led to the shul. Behind the shul was a grassy hill that slowed Marsha's steps. For here, just beyond the rise was the cemetery.

Tonight would be her last visit to Papa's grave. Since he had died, she made a daily visit, often at night so that Mama wouldn't say, "Enough already. Enough." At night she could read little poems or sing her songs. She was sure that Mama knew about her nighttime visits, for she often sighed, looked as if she wanted to say something, then turned away.

Papa rests there among relatives that only Mama remembered. When people die do they feel anything?

There was no one to answer that question. She longed to be a little girl again, small enough to crawl into her mother's bed. But her mother would pat her arm and feel her head for fever. Only Papa and she had shared thoughts about dying. Papa had never said there would be another world, but Marsha looking into his deep-set eyes had always felt that she could see into his soul. If that could happen while he was alive, who was to say that it couldn't happen after death? Mama often told her to keep her feet on the earth, not up in the clouds.

Even though a half moon guided her footsteps, Marsha had never felt so alone and sad. She was relieved when a neighbor's puppy followed her, ran on ahead and returned to lick her hand. She stepped carefully across the rocky paths between the graves. Papa's simple stone was gray now, changed forever by the wind and the rain from its sparkling whiteness that had so pleased her when the rabbi and the family gathered a year later for the unveiling of the headstone.

Marsha stretched herself out on top of Papa's grave. She dug her fingers into the tufts of grass and felt herself a part of the earth, the grass growing slowly all around her and even up through her body, green and fresh. She whispered, "You will be with me forever, Papa. I will remember your words and be true to your teachings. Your voice will be in my ears saying, 'The family, always the family, the family is everything.' " She placed a little poem under a rock. It would be there until the first rain. In the moonlight, the small trees surrounding the cemetery rustled in a breezeless night, and Marsha bent her head waiting for the touch of her Papa's hand to bless her for the long journey ahead.

Finally, holding the blanket closely to her chilled body, Marsha retraced her steps, looking up at the cloud that almost covered the moon. When she returned home, she found the place on the door where the mezuzah had been and left a kiss on the spot. Her sisters were sleeping deeply, and, grateful for their warmth, she slid into bed, pulling the quilt around herself and Nettie.

When she awoke, it was still dark, but the chill in the air told her that dawn was near. She heard her mother's worried voice, "Doctor, Harry feels very hot. Will he be able to make the journey? " Marsha's sleep had been so deep she had not heard the doctor come into their house.

"Mrs. Abrams, I can only give him some medicine now. Cover him lightly until the fever breaks. If he is hot again tomorrow, you will have to leave him with me until he is well enough to travel. There are people leaving the village every week, and we will find a family for him to travel with. If he is better, keep him warm; feed him with a little broth and cool water. No night air, please; his lungs are delicate."

Marsha heard Mama's tired voice, "May God give us the strength to make the journey a safe and healthy one for my children." Fully awake, Marsha stared at the still, shadowy ceiling. What would happen to Harry if he had to stay behind? He was her favorite brother, and the thought of his illness made her stomach knot with pain.

But in the morning, Harry looked better. Marsha said, "Please drink a little broth. It tastes delicious and you will need all your energy today. " She tried to sound more cheerful than she felt, and she smiled back at her mother whose approving eyes were upon her.

The friends and relatives, the rabbi, the teacher, and all the children stood near the road to say goodbye as the family piled into the dairy man's wagon, cleaned up for the occasion. Even his two black horses wore flowers around their necks. It didn't matter to the children that the wagon smelled strongly of milk nor that their only seats were wooden benches that the carpenter had put in place for them. With their packages and satchels piled around their feet, the family took their last look at the only home they had ever known, all of them quiet now, even little Goldie and Miriam who nestled in their mother's arms. Marsha wore her blue straw hat and glanced back once in the direction of the cemetery.

Her mother only looked to the road ahead. Her face was thoughtful when she spoke to her children. "We have had a good life here, but it is time to leave. The friends who stay behind may not be as lucky as we are." Marsha remembered the rabbi's warnings about the pogroms in the big cities and the danger to all the Jews wherever they lived. She put her arm around Harry and promised herself once again that she would take care of him.

Marsha knew that her mother was right. They had left Russia at a good time. But poor Harry was turned back at Ellis Island. The family thanked God that he was well enough to join them a year later when a cousin brought him to New York. He ran through the house, marveling at all the space and the view of the big street outside the window.

When Mama told me her stories, she also told me that she had a dream of a big fire sweeping through Horadisht, leaving nothing behind but charred wood and a few brick chimneys. She was sure the fire had really happened, but she prayed that her Papa's grave had not been disturbed. I was very quiet for a full hour, until I wanted something to nosh.

1933   Drinking Tea with Bubbie

As a child, I dreamed of having a large family, with lots of brothers and sisters. My wishes did not come true, but for a short while my family grew by accident. When I was eight years old, my family lived with Aunt Goldie and Uncle Seymore in Brooklyn. Their house was made of brick and had its own yard with trees and flowers, a wonder to me, knowing only the bare back yards of our apartment buildings. My brother told me it was because it was the Depression and we were poor. I didn't feel poor. It was fun to live with family, especially with my grandmother, Bubbie. Bubbie was my mother's mother, and I loved her. In a strange way, she was part of my nightlife; we had a secret.

Mama's family was the kind of family I always wanted, six sisters and three brothers. They chattered and moved quickly around Aunt Goldie's big dining room where we ate huge meals and sang songs at holidays. Bubbie was always the center of the family and managed to give everyone her attention, despite her inability to speak English. I loved to sit next to her on Friday nights when she would light the Sabbath lights, wave her hands around and say a prayer in Yiddish, which sounded mysterious and magical to me.

Bubbie and I had a special closeness that the rest of the family was unaware of. While everyone slept, I'd leave my bedroom, which changed with the coming of darkness to a place where exaggerated fears of monsters hiding in closets, and unnamed diseases lurked to destroy my peace of mind. Foremost amongst all my worries was a nagging fear about health.

I'd spend hours tossing and turning, opening and closing my mouth, positive that I had contracted lockjaw, a deadly disease our teacher had warned us about. The next morning when my jaws ached from the night's exertions, I was sure my life on earth was limited. Well, that is until I became obsessed with another disease.

One night, unable to sleep, I went to the kitchen looking for a glass of water and found Bubbie sitting at the kitchen table drinking tea from a heavy glass. I was fascinated by the way she grasped a spoon and pressed it against the edge of the glass while she sipped slowly with a sugar cube held between her teeth. I had time to watch her because she concentrated on blowing on the glass to cool the tea a little.

She looked so alone and tiny, wrapped up in an old blue bathrobe that probably belonged to Uncle Seymore. I had never noticed how pretty she was, or perhaps I didn't realize until then that old people could still be pretty. As she sat under the dim kitchen light, her skin looked as soft and smooth as Mama's. My fingers itched to travel down her delicate thin nose, different from Mama's and even from Aunt Goldie's. But her eyes were exactly like Mama's turning up as they did at the corners, and dark brown in color with little flecks of gold that picked up the shine from the light on her glasses. Mama, too, wore glasses, and I never realized how pretty she was either, since her glasses often hid the dancing of her eyes when she was amused.

It felt strange to stand there in the kitchen almost as if I were invisible and watch Bubbie. I resisted the temptation to speak, since I enjoyed seeing Bubbie this way. Her gray hair, pulled off her face and coiled into a bun at the back of her neck, reminded me of Mama's in its thinness, which let light shine through on her scalp. For a moment, I worried that I, too, would inherit their hair, but then Bubbie looked up and smiled.

She opened her arms, and I flew into them, safe at last from the fearful thoughts that crowded into my nighttime mind. "Hello, sweetheart," she said, using some of her very limited English. Then in Yiddish that I guessed at because of her worried face, she asked, "Are you sick?" I answered in English, "No, Bubbie, but I can't sleep."

I moved close to her chair, hoping she'd tell me to sit down. When she smiled at me again, I was surprised that she had no teeth. Her pink gums interested me, but I tried not to stare. Bubbie pulled out a deck of cards from a pocket in her robe. She motioned to me to sit down next to her and said, "Casino?" I nodded happily for she had taught me this game during the daylight hours after school.

After that night, I got used to drinking tea at midnight or later, for Bubbie assumed that tea was necessary to loving companionship. The first time we played Casino, she let me win the raisins and almonds we used instead of coins. Sometimes Bubbie would show me that I had more points than I realized. She didn't care about winning, and she knew that my arithmetic was not too good for I counted on my fingers.

After we played, she let me take out the big tortoise combs in her hair to allow the long fine strands to tumble down her back like a silver stream happy to be released. I reached for her brush and pretended to fix her hair for a special occasion. She pointed to my winnings and sang

"Rashinkes Mit Mandlen", a little song that Mama had taught me. In English it meant "Raisins and Almonds."

Once I had asked Mama, "Why can't Bubbie speak English?" I wanted to ask her so many questions. Did she still mourn for her husband, the Papa that Mama loved so much? What did she do when she was left all alone in Russia to take care of her children? But all we could do was smile and hug. That told me how much Bubbie loved me. I liked to rub my face against the sweet-smelling softness of her cheeks that reminded me of the roses my aunt planted in her garden.

Mama told me, "Bubbie never had to learn much English. When we first came to America, the family all spoke Yiddish. The people at temple speak Yiddish. She's perfectly happy." But I secretly longed to teach her so that we could really speak to each other during the hours that we shared alone. I wondered if she missed being in her own home in her little village.

I would take out my storybooks and point out pictures to her. "See, Bubbie, that's 'girl' and 'boy', 'mother' and 'father'". She'd put her hand covered with light brown spots over my hand as I said each word. I clapped when she was able to recognize the words, and she smiled her toothless grin. I never heard her speak those new words, but occasionally she'd point to a picture in the Yiddish paper she read and nod her head. We both understood and kept our secrets.

I was rarely confused when she spoke to me in Yiddish. Instinctively I knew that every night she said, "Be a good girl and help your Mama. I love you." I took her words with me as I slipped back into bed, unconcerned for the moment about the scary monsters or the new disease we had studied in school.

In my hand, I clutched the nickel she gave me as she kissed me goodnight. In her halting English, she always said, "Don't tell Mama." It was another secret.

I left her sitting in the kitchen with the overhead light shining on her gray hair. Usually she played solitaire, and I wondered when she was tired enough to go to sleep. Did old women all around the world play cards when they couldn't sleep? The thought comforted me.

I wished I could find a way to uncover Bubbie's memories. Now I realize how much I missed in my childhood because we only spoke the language of love. What was she thinking years later when she grew too old to play Casino or even to hold her own glass of tea? Mama told me she could only manage to hold her prayer book, but that often she'd just sit and stare out the window. I can imagine her thoughts:

It is no good to be so old. All day long I sit where a little light comes into these eyes that no longer can see the words of God. Why did He take away my sight? What do I have left? Daughter Goldie is good to me. She bathes me, helps me dress, but she gets upset when I complain. Everything hurts. I don't want to wear the teeth the dentist made, so I don't eat much of the food Goldie made for me.

I want to remember the years when I was young and strong. All my children listened to me, not like today. We sang, lit the candles on Shabbos, and the children always begged for a piece of my homemade challah. What a sweet smell; oi, if I only had my own teeth for just a few minutes!

My dear husband, such a sweet and gentle man, yet he walked with his head in the clouds. Books, books, always the Torah or the Talmud. The boys had to help him in the tailoring shop or else we would have trouble putting food on the table. And my little daughter, Marsha, so like her Papa. Her hand was always in his, her eyes on his face. She even tried to walk like him, sometimes with her hands behind her back and her eyes all squinted, pretending to be thinking such big ideas.

It makes me cry even now to think how young he was when dear God took him from us. Little Marsha was sick for at least two weeks. The town doctor said we might lose her, too. Such crying, such sadness. I thought she'd never stop.

How I missed my husband, but the children helped so much. That's when they talked about going to America every night as we drank our tea around the old samovar. What a dream they had. Only Marsha screamed that she wouldn't leave the village where Papa lay in the cemetery. Dear Alice took care of Marsha as she always did when I had the youngest to feed or put down to sleep. Such a good sister. Like a little mother she was.

Sometimes, God forgive me, I even cried out to my husband, "Why did you leave me? So many children, so many mouths to feed."

And now, I can hardly see my children's faces. At least I can remember the good years. Soon, soon, I hope to be with my husband again. God willing.

I'm not like Bubbie, for like most of my friends in California where we live, I only speak English. I have one little grandson who has just turned five. Jeremy makes my heart jump when he says, "Grandma....." It doesn't matter what he asks for; I will give it to him. When he is a little older, I will tell him about my Bubbie, and perhaps I will remember enough of Casino to teach it to him. He doesn't know Jack, his father's Dad, who died before he had the joy of holding Jeremy in his arms. I will tell him all the stories about this grandfather and his own Dad. Perhaps I will make a video and tell him my life story, too. My mother told me her stories about Russia, her beloved Papa, and her clan of sisters and brothers. I have one dear brother, but Jeremy will hear our stories as well. It feels good to think about Jeremy watching our family history. It feels good, too, to use my imagination and pretend that I have a big family like Mama's.

But in so many ways I do, for now that I am a grandma myself, I can bring my aunts and uncles out of my memories. Bubbie comes alive again, and I can almost feel her soft hands touching mine as she deals the cards for Casino.

1938 "Don't Worry--I'll Be All Right"

So much was happening during these years. The family spoke of the gathering war clouds over Europe, and the newspapers made my father worry the most. He loved to read about history and would tell me stories about terrible wars in the past and how lucky he was not to have been called to fight in WWI. He came down with the terrible influenza that took the lives of thousands of people. He worried aloud, but I hugged all my fears to my breast just as I had in the days when I lived with Bubbie.

In fact, I spent my growing up years worrying. What I worried about was not war or floods or even the escape of the lions from the nearby zoo. I worried about health, Mama's, Daddy's, and my own. Perhaps it goes back to my early years in the Bronx.

Our living room was large and comfortable with overstuffed chairs that had bright red, green, and yellow slipcovers. But it held a secret that made it special. Daddy always brought medicine home from his pharmacy and stored it in the drawers of the living room tables when there was no more room in the bathroom cabinets. I knew that most people didn't have medicine in their living room. I liked to open the drawers and poke around trying to learn the names of the pills, potions, and powders wrapped in little paper packets. Daddy enjoyed teaching me the difficult words.

Unfortunately, Daddy had high blood pressure. He didn't talk about it, but I got used to seeing him, ensconced in his big leather chair, counting his pulse, one finger poised on his wrist. "Are you Okay?" I asked.

"Don't worry. I'm fine."

One day he fainted in the hot shower just as I came home from school. I only caught a glimpse of Mama and my brother Michael supporting him as he climbed out of the slippery old tub, clutching the heavy shower curtain. "The shower was too hot," he called out to me, "I'll be all right." His bare feet looked so white on the floor with the tiny black and white tiles. I didn't like to see him with bare feet. Mama's lips so tight and rigid were almost as white as Daddy's bare feet.

Mama had health problems, too. Most of the time she worked doing everything to keep the house neat and our family well fed. One day she admitted that she felt quite ill and stayed in bed. Late in the evening, she called out to me, "Run down to the corner candy store and call Dr. Goldberg. Tell him that the medicine he told me to take is making me feel worse."

I hated to leave Mama, but we didn't have a phone. All our calls were made at the candy store down the block. I ran all the way, and for once I had no desire for the chocolates or the halvah that usually made my mouth water. By the time I reached the doctor on the store phone, I was crying so hard that I could barely give him the message.

"Stop crying, foolish girl. Tell her to take the medicine only in the morning. She had a reaction to the sulfa. Don't worry. She'll be all right." Dr. Goldberg took care of our family, and he knew me very well. He also knew that he had to be stern with me or I'd never stop crying.

Most of the time I didn't worry about Mama's health. She was an expert at washing and cleaning and a wonderful cook, a balabusta at choosing the freshest vegetables, and a magician at knowing which chicken had just breathed its last breath. Above all, she was the arbiter of all that was good and just. "Did you get one hundred percent on your test?" That's what Mama meant by good. When I got a stomach ache because I ate too many cookies, Mama said, "You get punished when you are greedy." That was just!

To me, Mama was love, but I had to work hard to earn it. Daddy was safety, and smelled faintly of pharmaceuticals, but Mama smelled of warm milk and bread and cookies and chocolate cake. Her busy figure, wrapped in an apron, made me feel the stability of the earth beneath my feet. But when Mama was sick, my world spun around like the globe that Daddy loved to investigate.

One night I tried to bribe my brother to do my homework for me. "So what can you give me?" he asked, knowing very well that I had no instant source of funds.

"Maybe Mama can give me an advance on my allowance."

He looked up quickly. "Better leave her alone. She's not feeling so hot." He returned to his own homework.

His words put me on instant alert. I went looking for Mama and found her sitting on her favorite chair in the living room. Its tall back, lined with dark velvet, made her look like a queen. But when Mama sat still with nothing in her hands to do, I knew something was wrong. Her face was pale, and her eyes behind her round glasses were dull and unseeing. She kept one hand pressed to her side while the other held her Bible, both reasons for me to worry. "Can I help you, Mama?" I stood by her chair anxiously hoping she would scold me for leaving my homework, or at least show that she knew I existed. I stroked her arm and kissed her cheek.

"Leave me alone now, my daughter. I just need to rest. The pain will go away and I'll be fine."

Instead of listening to her words, I watched her face, which usually told a different story. Daddy said that Mama had trouble with her gall bladder, and I added that to my list of terrible diseases that could carry my mother away from me. I spent hours in the library looking up gall bladder disease as well as Uncle Harry's tuberculosis. From the books, I could see that tuberculosis was more dangerous, but Mama refused to have surgery. Maybe she was in as much danger as Uncle Harry was. My dreams were full of big words in books so heavy that they hurt my hands to hold them.

"I can make you a nice cup of tea," I ventured. In my family, tea and chicken soup became love offerings when anyone was sick.

"Thank you, darling, I'll be all right." Again those words. But a sudden pain must have struck, for she bent over and gasped.

Filled with helplessness, I went back to my studying, but the numbers danced crazily before my eyes. Instead I heard Mama's voice in my head telling me her old story about her Papa and how he had died in her arms when she was only nine years old. I can still hear the sorrow in her voice. Try to imagine a very little girl bent over her father's bed:

"Papa, speak to me, please Papa," Marsha cried as she tugged at his nightshirt, so damp from his sweat that Marsha felt her own skin grow moist.

"Marsha dear, Papa is looking at you," her mother said. "He wants to tell you something."

"Papa, I am here. I will never leave you until you are well again."

His cracked lips opened and closed as his breath came in uneven ragged gasps. Then Marsha heard his weak voice, so soft she had to lean over to understand his words. "Remember, sweet girl, remember what I taught you." He struggled once more for breath. "You will be the one to keep the family together." Another pause and then, "The family, the family, my little Marsha. Nothing must hurt the family."

Tears streamed down Marsha's face. She rested her head on her father's arm and fell into an exhausted sleep. Later she heard that her older sisters, Alice and Hester, had carried her to bed. They told her that she had been crying hysterically and struggling to go back to her Papa.

Her sisters decided that they had better call the village doctor, who was taking care of Papa. Brother Harry rushed to the other side of the village to get him. When they arrived at the house, the doctor touched his fingers to the mezuzzah on the front door. He greeted the family and gave his black wool hat to Alice who was his favorite.

"So now it's Marsha who gets an old man out of his bed." He followed Alice to Marsha's bed, opened his bag, and pulled out a stethoscope. "Hm, hmm," he said as he moved his instrument over Marsha's chest. Marsha continued to sleep as his fingers tapped while he leaned his head down to listen. "She needs air to breathe. Let's open the window. Now take me to your Mama," the doctor told Alice. "You must insist on absolute rest, Mrs. She is too young to be sitting up nights with little sleep."

"And my husband?"

"I am sorry. He will not last the night. May the Lord rest his soul. There's nothing I can do for him now."

The sisters took turns watching over their father as he slipped deeper into a coma. When he died, they left their mother alone to grieve by his bedside, whispering the prayers she knew by heart and holding her husband's hand.

Though they were very tired, the girls went to care for little Marsha, who slept for another day and night. When their Mama woke, she smiled at her children and said, "Papa would not want us to worry. We'll be all right."

Mama was no longer that little girl, and it was *I* who worried and tried to pray. When Mama's pain forced her to moan, I hurried to her side and she answered my anxious questions. She attempted a little smile and said, "It's much better. Don't worry."

Don't worry? Mama so tired, so pale--might as well tell me not to breathe. How could I study? I watched, bit my nails and wondered what it would be like in a world without Mama.

1939   Listening to Family Secrets

The family made me nervous talking about the danger of the United States getting involved in the big war in Europe. I listened and listened. I hoped the World's Fair wouldn't be affected!

I knew from the time I was little that I wanted to be a writer. It was easy to listen in to family gossip and make up stories in my head. I'd be really quiet, and my mother and her sisters usually forgot that I was there. The stories I made up were mostly true, but even then I had the imagination of the writer I became. I can close my eyes and be with the aunts again. Yes, I can see them now....

Aunt Goldie, Mama, and Aunt Nettie are washing and drying the dishes after the usual Sunday dinner. It's comfortable in Aunt Goldie's big kitchen, which has always been my favorite spot to read while the aunts gossip and talk "women talk." The fact that they ignore me doesn't bother me at all. Maybe they think that people that read can't hear. Very few of the aunts and uncles do more than pick up the daily paper and scan the headlines. If they knew that one day I would write down everything I heard, they would be angry...

The uncles and cousins, mostly male, sprawl in groaning comfort in the living room. Aunt Miriam's tinkling laughter contrasts with the boom-boom of the male voices. She rarely joins her sisters in the after dinner clean up.

"That foolish Miriam," Aunt Goldie says, scrubbing a big copper pot, "She spends all her money on makeup and clothes. One of these days Bernie will find out she uses her household allowance to gamble. Believe me, there will be trouble."

Aunt Nettie shrugs her shoulders and adds, "If she gets caught it's her own fault. Money drips through her fingers. No one has any to spare in these hard times. You'd think she didn't know there's a Depression."

Mama, always the peacemaker, moves away from stacking the dishes to be closer to her sisters. "She's so pretty and lighthearted. Everyone has always treated her like a precious child. We better not talk about Miriam. If her Bernie finds out..." She doesn't finish the sentence, but I already know that Uncle Bernie has a bad temper.

Aunt Goldie turns to Mama and asks, "Did she ever tell you that Bernie hits her?"

"Shush," Mama says, "Do you want the children to hear?"

Aunt Nettie clicks her tongue in disapproval. "If my Marvin put a hand on me, I'd walk out with the kids."

"Sure," Aunt Goldie says, "and then you'd move in with me."

Aunt Nettie gets caught up in their game and continues, "Of course Marvin would come after me, and we'd all end up playing poker for the night." Mama joins in the laughter too, though she and Daddy never play cards.

I slip out of the warm kitchen, glad they haven't noticed my departure. What a lot to think about. What does Aunt Miriam do when she gambles? It was a new word to me. Do men really hit their wives?

When I walk into the front room, Aunt Miriam is dancing to the music on the phonograph, and Uncle Marvin is teasing her by pulling on her apron strings. Aunt Miriam's lips and eyes shine as she twirls away. Uncle Bernie sits quietly in one of the soft chairs, smoking and watching. I can't help looking at his hands. Then I look away, my heart beating so quickly that I'm afraid someone will notice my red face.

A week later, Sunday dinner is quite different. The aunts and uncles eat rapidly. All I hear is the slurping when they eat their soup. Their silence makes my cousins and me jumpy and silly. I wonder what is going on. I notice that Aunt Miriam's eyes are so red and puffy that even her makeup can't hide the damage. Uncle Bernie refills his wine glass so often that Uncle Marvin says, "Hey, Bernie, leave some for the rest of us."

Uncle Bernie jumps up from his chair and marches to a back bedroom. When Aunt Miriam follows him, I remember what the aunts said last week. Curiosity makes me want to investigate, though I know Mama would be upset. Nobody notices me leaving, so busy are they making noise to relax the nervous feeling we all have.

I stand in the hallway and hear Aunt Miriam's voice, "Bernie, you can't tell me what to do every minute of the day. You spy on me as if I were a criminal. I don't steal the food money and you know it."

Uncle Bernie's shouts make me shrink against the wall, wishing I hadn't dared to follow him and Aunt Miriam.

"Either you stop this crazy gambling or I'll throw you out of the house!"

Suddenly Uncle Bernie bursts out of the doorway with Aunt Miriam following close behind, both arguing without concern for who can hear them. He shoves me out of his way as he makes a dash for the front door. Why on earth is Aunt Miriam slapping away at his back with her purse?

I am so upset that I remain sitting alone for the rest of the evening. Mama and the aunts are wrong. It was Aunt Miriam doing the hitting. I chew on my nails until I make one finger bleed. I stare at the blood and begin to worry about blood poisoning.

That night I can't sleep because I worry about the family. I have always felt so secure and happy with them. This sudden change shakes me out of my story book existence. If I can't be sure of their love for one another, what can I be sure of? Mama always said her family believed in love. When I can't sleep, I try to write in my journal. I hide it among all the magazines that Mama calls "trashy".

I am in for another rude awakening a few weeks later. The family, except for Aunt Miriam and Uncle Bernie, pile into two cars and head for a picnic at Coney Island. What fun it is to hear the kids shout as they dash into the ocean. I love the tangy salt air that tickles my nostrils. While Mama and the aunts pull chicken sandwiches, potato salad, meat loaf, and honey cake from their paper sacks, I busy myself in the sand creating castles and moats for the characters in my books that I will write, if only in my head. I would give all my lunch money if Mama would buy me an old typewriter.

As usual, the aunts give quick hugs and a pinch on my cheek and promptly forget that I exist.

"Alice called today," Mama says. "Brother Sam's Alice."

"Well, Marsha, what did she have to say?" Aunt Nettie asks.

Mama looks around her, but I seem to be invisible to her. Then she whispers, "Alice thinks Sam has a... a woman. Someone from the shop."

Aunt Goldie sucks in her breath. "Sam is such a good man, a good father. Why would she think that?" For a minute I think Aunt Goldie is going to cry. Sam is her favorite brother, even though he lives so far away in the Bronx. To my family, Brooklyn is another country compared to the Bronx.

"Well," Mama says, "Alice tells me he comes home late every night and won't tell her where he's been. She's so upset..." Mama looks ready to join Aunt Goldie in a sisterly cry.

I slide away from their little huddled group and pretend to build up the sides of my castle, all the while chewing over this new family crisis. What does it mean to " have a woman"? Aunt Alice was a woman. Why were the aunts so upset?

Mama worries a lot, and already I think I'm just like her. Aunt Goldie tells me I read too much. My anxiety finally forces me to turn to my older brother Michael, who generally ignores me unless he's dumping pepper in my soup.

"No kidding? Aunt Miriam hit Uncle Bernie and Uncle Sam has a woman? It's about time we had some excitement in this family. These Sunday dinners bore me to death."

"But," I squeak plaintively, "What's going to happen to us?"

"To us? Nothing. We'll just keep visiting and fooling around every week. You'll see. The aunts will go back to gossiping and act like nothing's happened."

He was right, of course. But I was never the same little girl after that. What I assumed to be as strong as a rock was as shaky as the orange Jell-O mold that Aunt Goldie prepared every Sunday.

I was growing up, even learning to hide things I didn't want Mama to know. One of my friends finally told me what it meant to "have a woman." By then, I wasn't too shocked.

I don't want to worry about the family any more. But the child in me wants to return to that big warm kitchen, to hear the uncles telling jokes or snoring after dinner. I wish I could hear the aunts boasting about their beautiful, wonderful children. It would be fun to be invisible one more time. Writing all the stories down will make me remember them forever. The trouble is that they will no longer just be mine.

MAMA CONTROLS OUR WORLD

1939 Mama Rescues Uncle Saul

I stared at the pictures of Mama's young brothers who sat on the front porch of their Brooklyn house grinning for the camera. "Uncle Saul looks just like Uncle Harry."

Mama smiled as she glanced over at the album spread out on the kitchen table. She wiped her wet hands on her apron before sitting down next to me. "Oh my! That's such an old picture, taken before Uncle Harry got sick and moved to California—and before Uncle Saul moved to Philadelphia. I miss him very much."

"It's sad that he moved so far. Why did he have to leave Brooklyn?"

Mama's shrug and the clicking sound she made with her tongue when she pushed the album away ended our rare moment of relaxation together. "I have so much to do before dinner, and you, my daughter, have left your homework for the last minute."

When Mama's voice closed down like the dropping of an iron gate, I knew it would be useless to ask any more questions. So I was startled that evening when Mama received a phone call from Ruth, Uncle Saul's wife, all the way from Philadelphia. Because we still found a telephone to be somewhat of a miracle, everyone stopped to listen, even Daddy who had telephones in his drug store. Before Mama picked up the receiver, she breathed a worried prayer, "Please God, don't let there be trouble."

I always felt that Mama had a special relationship with God, but this time her puzzled face told a different story. She only spoke a few times, gradually becoming more and more agitated. "Calm down, Ruth. Don't yell in my ear." Then, "How can you be sure?" And finally, "All right, all right. I'll come but only for the weekend."

Mama put down the receiver and swiveled around to face Daddy, Michael, and me. Daddy rattled his newspaper impatiently and said, "Well?" My brother and I kept quiet. We knew this was grown-up business, but we, too, expected Mama to share the news.

She sat down next to Daddy's big chair, slowly untying her apron strings. She turned her head toward me and said, "I'm taking you with me, Carole, to visit Uncle Saul and Aunt Ruth." Her voice was calm, but her fingers twisted the apron strings into an untidy mess.

While I was digesting her statement, Mama spoke to Daddy, who had dropped his paper to the carpet near his chair. "Please, no arguments. Ruth said there's a …problem." I knew that Daddy would get the details when he and Mama were alone. I also knew why Mama needed me. She never discussed her inability to understand printed directions when she traveled. I played the part of companion and discreet helper. Like, "Ask the conductor which train to take and what platform it stops at."

The day we left, Mama packed chicken and fruit for the long train ride while I tried to think of some way to ask why we were going. "Never mind the questions, my daughter. Just put the clothes I set out into the black suitcase from under the bed."

Mama and I arrived in Philadelphia tired but anxious to greet Uncle Saul who waited for us at the station. He wrapped his arms around Mama and I could hear him say, "Ruth is meshuga. She's driving me crazy with her foolish notions. I'm glad you're here, Marsha dear." He kissed me and pinched my cheek. "You are such a young lady now. Be careful or you'll have all the boys running after you."

I could feel the warmth rush into my face and ducked my head to hide my embarrassment. Mama laughed and hugged her brother again. "Always talking about such silly things. Carole is only fourteen. Don't put such nonsense into her head."

When Uncle Saul led us up the steps to his front door, all the laughter stopped. I had enough time to notice that his small wooden house shared one wall with his neighbor. Mama told me on the train that Uncle Saul lived in a row house. Now I understood what that meant. But why did Aunt Ruth take so long to answer the doorbell? Did she have to walk down a long narrow hallway?

Meanwhile, Uncle Saul said, "Sorry dears, but I rushed out to the station and forgot my keys." Suddenly the door opened with such a whoosh that Uncle Saul lost his balance and almost fell into the dark hallway. Aunt Ruth ignored him but opened her arms to Mama and me saying, "Come in, come in. You both look wonderful." Uncle Saul fumbled with the doorknob and finally followed us in.

I hung on to Mama's hand for I felt suddenly shy in this strange house in a city I had never visited before. Uncle Saul struggled up the stairs with a suitcase in each hand. How funny, I thought, those suitcases have so few things in them that even I was able to carry them without any trouble. But then Uncle Saul was older than Mama.

Later at dinner, we sat in the tiny kitchen with our elbows touching since the round yellow table barely fit into the room once all four of us sat down to eat. Usually, I'd enjoy the closeness of a family dinner, but tonight I could sense a nagging discomfort in the room that made the kitchen seem even smaller. The atmosphere was so unpleasant that the grown-ups looked like people sitting around the bed of a dying person.

Aunt Ruth's hands flew nervously to her hair to push a straggling curl back under the hairnet she wore. When she had no success, she dug some bobby pins into the offending hair with such force that left a red track across her forehead. Mama worked to lighten the mood, "You should see Goldie's new apartment, all decorated like a Hollywood palace." Her eyes darted from Aunt Ruth, who only pushed the food around on her plate, to Uncle Saul, who didn't eat a bite. He sat with a foolish smile on his face while his eyes blinked every few seconds.

Mama startled me by asking me to recite a poem in French! I squeaked out an apologetic, "I can't. I need Michael to help me with the lines." It was the truth, but Mama made me feel like a traitor. Her eyes sent a message I had no trouble reading: You have failed me. When I spilled my root beer on the floor, however, she relented and cleaned up the mess after giving my hand a quick squeeze.

Uncle Saul gulped down his very hot tea and excused himself, saying, "I will see you in the morning. My boss asked me for a special favor. He needs his suit altered for his son's wedding. When a boss asks, how can I say no?" He shrugged his shoulders and left in a big hurry.

It was a good thing he did. When the door slammed, Aunt Ruth burst into tears and Mama rushed over to rock her in her arms the way she used to hold me when I hurt myself. "Sha, sha, Ruthie. It will be all right." Then she added in a no-nonsense tone, "Go upstairs, Carole, and hang up our clothes. Read your book but turn off the light at ten o'clock."

I opened my mouth to protest but decided against it. I did manage to walk up the steps very slowly and heard Aunt Ruth wailing, "Saul doesn't go to the shop, Marsha. He runs every night to his girlfriend." Then after a long sob, I heard, "To his shiksa."

Upstairs, I turned and twisted in bed for rat least two hours, praying that Mama would come upstairs and hold me, too. Aunt Ruth's last word hung in the air with red jagged lines all around it. A "shiksa"! No one in our family had ever been involved with a person who wasn't a Jew. And now, Mama's oldest brother had brought disgrace to the family. I gnawed at my nails. What will happen next?

I tried to push out a few tears, but all I managed were both a hearty sneeze and a huge sigh. I felt better, but I really wanted something more dramatic to happen. It did. Uncle Saul came home, and I awoke from a fitful sleep to shouting and crying.

Nothing could keep me in that room. Not even imagining Mama's frown if she were to see me. I peeked out into the empty hall at the top of the stairs, crouched down, hugged my cold knees and tried to stop my chattering teeth. "Mama, "I whispered to myself, "make them stop yelling."

"You are an old fool!" Aunt Ruth shouted. "That woman thinks she will get this house if she gets you! She'll have to wait 'till I die." I heard glass shattering on the floor. Mama's low, soothing voice didn't stop the argument.

"At least she listens to me, understands how I feel and doesn't call me names. A man wants a woman who's proud of him! You treat me like a piece of furniture: keep me clean, push me around, and hardly remember that I'm here!"

"Proud of you? I should be proud? I had to pull you away from all those sisters of yours. Always telling you how wonderful you were-- a regular prince!"

For the first time Mama spoke loudly, "Ruth, do you know what you are saying in front of me?" Mama sounded shocked but not angry. Puzzled, I inched my way down the steps; when they creaked, I froze. The noise from the parlor continued. Nobody thought about me and for this I thanked God.

Aunt Ruth paused for a minute to answer Mama, "I never meant you, Marsha, only your other sisters. When I met your brother, I hated to go into that big house. I knew I wasn't as pretty as your sisters, but Saul said he loved me."

I couldn't hear anything for a few seconds, then my uncle spoke. "Once long ago I loved you." There was sorrow in my uncle's voice and I wanted to see his face. I moved down a few more steps and peeked around the end of the banister. Aunt Ruth sat like a sack of wet wash back from the laundry. Uncle Saul stood near Mama who sat straight and very tall.

Mama and Uncle Saul, close together but not touching, left a yawning space between them and my weeping aunt. Uncle Saul spoke to Aunt Ruth again, this time after placing his hand on my mother's shoulder. "Don't think I didn't know you tricked me into moving away from my family."

Mama tilted her head sharply to see Uncle Saul's face. I could tell she was waiting for his next words, for her chest barely moved. He continued, "You told me we had to move to Philadelphia so you could get your share of your father's will--this house."

We all saw Aunt Ruth as she sat up in her chair. The tears left wet smudges of rouge on her face--almost like the pictures of clowns I had on my bedroom wall. Her eyes had hardened into two black marbles. She spoke in a voice so different from those eyes that I had to watch her mouth to see if the words were really coming from her. Then I recognized the voice; it was my own when I wanted something special from Daddy or was trying to beg Mama to let me go to the movies.

Aunt Ruth said, "That was the truth, Saul. As God is my witness. Why would I lie to you?" She turned first to my uncle and then to Mama, spread out her hands, and protested her innocence. "My older sister refused to sell the house which my father left to both of us. You remember. She said it was our family's home and that we had to come here and live with her until she died."

"Yes, Ruthie, and you made me miserable every day of our married life. Always saying it was 'your' house, and I only had certain privileges. For that you persuaded me to leave my family."

When I glanced at Mama, I jumped. A tiny smile flickered over her face and then disappeared behind the serious, concerned expression she had worn before. Mama, I thought, why does the fight make you smile?

Aunt Ruth's voice rose to a near shriek, "All right, so I had to drag you away from your sisters who licked your boots. 'Saulie darling, what a beautiful suit you're wearing,' 'Saulie, sweetheart, you have such lovely hair. I wish my hair looked like yours.' But after all these years when I've tried to be a good wife, you run to a shiksa! God should only strike you dead!"

My hand flew to my mouth. Nobody spoke like that in our family. Suddenly that woman was an outsider; how could she be my aunt? Mama stood up and walked--no marched--over to her sister-in-law. "How dare you say that to my brother? You are an evil woman." Mama, only 5'3" tall, towered over Ruth, her words striking and slashing in their fury. "You begged me to come here to help you. I left my home and took my child with me on a long trip, all out of the goodness of my heart."

Ruth crumpled and said, "Please, Marsha, you are the only one in the family that treated me nice. Saul loves and respects you. Won't you tell your brother that he must honor me as his wife?"

I watched many expressions float over Mama's face, one after another, like dark clouds in a threatening sky. Finally she spoke, "Very well. I came here to keep my family together. You sinned when you asked God to curse my brother, but...." She turned to Uncle Saul, who suddenly hung his head like a naughty child in front of his elder, "You, my brother, are also wrong, and your sin is greater than Ruth's. You must promise never to see that woman again."

I held my breath. Uncle Saul's meek voice didn't surprise me. "I promise. Ruth, I will give up my friend, but.... " His voice gained strength. He glanced at Mama, who nodded. "You must also promise to treat me like the man of this house, no more cruel names, no more nasty words."

Ruth breathed softly, "I promise, Saul. And thank you, dear Marsha." Mama simply nodded graciously.

I scuttled back up the steps, dove into bed and turned to the wall. What a night! I pretended to be asleep when I heard Mama come softly into the room. I'll have to tell Michael all about this excitement, I thought. Maybe he can explain why Mama was humming as she climbed into bed next to me. Well, I knew that Mama liked to win.

1940   Uncle Harry Leaves New York

Sure there was a war going on in Europe, and some of our merchant ships were sunk in the Atlantic, but it all seemed so far away when there were more pressing problems in the family.

It was a sultry summer day, the type of weather that makes New Yorkers groan. I was about thirteen and full of complaints as I dragged myself into the apartment, pulling up short when I saw the Brooklyn part of Mama's family milling around the living room.

"What's going on?" I asked my brother, who lounged against the freestanding bookcase as he kept a watchful eye on Mama.

"It's a mess. Mama's hysterical because Uncle Harry has to go to Denver."

"How come? And why is Mama so hysterical?" I followed my question by sticking my fingers into my mouth, an old habit that brought me dire warnings from Mama about the consequences of infected cuticles. Before

Michael could answer, I moved closer to Mama and the aunts to listen to the shrill conversation.

"Marsha, stop carrying on like Theda Bara. Harry has to go to Denver where there are specialists. Who's going to help him in the Bronx - your Dr. Goldberg?" Aunt Goldie scolded.

Mama sat up in her tall, antique chair, turned indignantly to her sister and said, "And why not? Dr. Goldberg is no fool. He took good care of my Carole when she had pneumonia, didn't he?"

Aunt Nettie pursed her little lips and chimed in, "Don't be silly. Carole's a strong girl. She probably would have recovered all by herself without the help of Dr. Goldberg, God willing." She pulled me to her and I felt smothered by her large bosom. I was crazy about most of Mama's sisters, but they all forgot that I was growing up fast. The uncles hadn't forgotten. I told my best friend, "Jeez, my uncles squeeze me so hard, I think they enjoy feeling my breasts against their chests." That was pretty racy for a fourteen-year-old.

Aunt Miriam also hugged me, but she didn't make me feel like a baby. While she kept her arm around me, she joined in the discussion, "The worst thing is that Harry has to leave his family. That's sad." Aunt Miriam secretly tickled me under the arm. She was rarely serious, loving dancing and playing cards more than heavy family discussions. Even so, Aunt Goldie was my favorite aunt of the five, and Aunt Nettie was next because I loved playing with my two cousins at her house.

Mama looked around to get everyone's attention and said, "If Harry was smart, he'd make Marilyn go with him. She's a good-looking woman, and who knows what can happen when a woman stays alone." Mama looked as if she knew the possibilities. The aunts nodded solemn agreement.

I heard the little sucking sound Aunt Nettie made with her tongue behind her teeth. It was her way to get attention. "What an awful thought. We should all take turns calling her every day." She glanced over at her husband, peacefully smoking his cigarette. Aunt Nettie looked nervous and flushed.

I needed to talk to Mama. I wiggled out of Aunt Miriam's arm and leaned against Mama's chair. "Why does Uncle Harry have to go to Denver and where is Denver anyhow?"

Mama paused for a second before answering, brushing my straight, dark hair out of my eyes and fixing my barrette. Then she said, "You'd think you'd learn that in school. Denver is in Colorado and Uncle Harry has to go to a hospital high in the mountains. They have important doctors there, really big men who know about tuberculosis." I could see that Mama was on the verge of crying, so I rolled the long word around in my mouth and kept quiet. Later, I'd ask Daddy about the disease. If Dr. Goldberg couldn't help Uncle Harry, it must be pretty serious.

The heat created little rivers on everyone's forehead, rivers that the patient family ignored. We were all used to New York summers. But Mama's pale, drawn face made me run to my dresser drawer in the room that my brother and I shared. I kept a pretty, flower-covered fan there that my friends and I had picked up in a musty store in Chinatown.

I rushed back into the living room where my aunts and uncles drooped in exhausted silence. No air moved in the room. "Here, Mama, use my fan." I pushed the wooden handle into her fingers, and she smiled a special smile. When Mama smiled at me like that, it was better than all the gold stars I tried to earn.

Uncle Sam, Mama's big, tall brother, spoke up from the depths of a chintz-covered chair that we kept near the only window in the room. When Daddy was home from the pharmacy, Michael and I never dared to sit in that chair. Daddy hated the heat even more than I did. "So," Uncle Sam grunted, "where will Harry get the money to pay for that hospital in Denver?"

Everyone stared at the floor. Times were still bad. The Depression, our teachers told us, still hung on and no one had any extra money. Mama spoke up, "Harry saved for a long time. Do you remember how he used to put away a few kopecks even as a young boy in Russia? Even when he had to go back to Russia when we got to Ellis Island, he still tried to save." Mama shook her head. I could see tears shining behind her gold-rimmed glasses.

Mama seemed to be able to live in the past as well as the present. Even her sisters were amazed at her memory. "Maybe," Aunt Goldie said as the others nodded their heads, "Maybe he knew that someday he would need a lot of money if the disease came back." Mama stood up slowly, smoothing her cotton dress, still crisp despite the humidity that made the curtains hang limply in the still air. She walked into her bedroom that was separated from the living room by glass doors. Curious, I followed her. She went to her low, mahogany dressing table and opened the top drawer. She looked at me with her special look. "Remember, my daughter, this is no place for your fingers unless I say so."

Mama knew that one of my delights was to snoop around in her dresser drawers to open and close the pretty jewelry boxes, some that Uncle Bernard, Daddy's brother, had brought back from Paris. It was nice to smell the handkerchiefs that Mama kept near her perfume bottles...but the top drawer was out of bounds to me.

Mama pulled out a small brown purse with a clasp so loose, she had to use a rubber band to keep it tightly shut. Only Mama opened that purse. Inside, she kept letters that Uncle Harry gave her as well as what she said were instructions for her will. I didn't like the sound of that word.

She carefully held some of the papers. They looked heavy and important, with typed letters and a fancy gold stamp on some of them. She put the other papers as far back as they would go then gave me her special look. When she returned to her chair in the living room, even Michael moved away from the bookcase to join the rest of the family. The family knew that Mama and Uncle Harry were the closest of all. Before he got so sick, they'd sit together in our house or his and talk quietly, their long, narrow heads so alike, her fine features matching his.

"This," said Mama importantly, "is all the information Harry asked me to keep about his money. He also gave me bonds to hold for him, every one of them bought with the money he earned downtown in the clothing lofts."

Aunt Nettie sighed, "Too bad he has to use the money to pay doctor bills. Better he should have some pleasure or save it for Arthur's schooling."

Everyone nodded. Uncle Harry had only one child. He was a few years younger than I, so I saw him only at big family picnics or parties. I felt terrible that he would have no Daddy around while Uncle Harry was far away in Denver.

"Someday," Mama stopped, her eyes looking out the window, "I'll have to be the one to take care of Harry's will." No one answered; they knew that Uncle Harry's disease would probably shorten his life though they never spoke about it in front of Bubbie, who had lost her husband as well as two tiny babies before the family came to America.

When the aunts whispered about death, this made me nervous and anxious. I often wanted to talk to Mama about Uncle Harry's disease, but it was hard to ask her questions that would make her sad.

Mama put three of the bonds into Uncle Sam's hands. "Here, take these to the bank and get cash for them. Harry will need them as soon as he gets to Denver." Then she lost control of her emotions, so carefully held down while she discussed the necessary money business. Uncle Sam held her close, while the other uncles looked away and the aunts dabbed at their eyes with their handkerchiefs.

No one cried like Mama who, while the most outspoken of the sisters, also dealt with life's setbacks as if each were a nail in her own coffin. Michael went over to Mama and kissed her. "Don't cry, Mama. Uncle Harry will get better in the hospital. Don't make yourself sick." Michael and Mama had a special closeness that I despaired of ever having. As her first child and a precious son, she always treated him differently, and the whole family realized it.

I stared at the little brown purse and suddenly hated it. I wanted to rip it from Mama's hands and burn it in the gas oven. It seemed to be the reason for the heat, for Mama's tears, and for the grateful hug she gave my brother.

I realized Mama's eyes were on me. Guiltily I stopped chewing on my nails. Even in her grief, Mama watched me, judged me, and silently molded me into the good daughter she expected me to be. The sweat ran down my face, tickled my nose, and dripped into my mouth. I was afraid to lick the drops from the end of my nose as my brother and I liked to do, daring each other to stick out our tongues as far as possible.

"Mama has eyes in the back of her head," I often complained to Michael, who'd laugh and agree. I secretly thought that Mama never expected him to be as perfect as she expected me to be. Maybe it was because Michael was named after her Papa and was tall the way Mama remembered her father to be. I was chubby and looked more like Daddy's family, with dark hair and very dark brown eyes.

The silence deepened. The aunts sighed heavily. The
uncles closed their eyes and dozed. The peddlers in the
yard shouted out their wares. Mama's tears flowed
endlessly as Uncle Sam patted her back.

I yawned and thought of the good book I was dying to
start.

1941   Bubbie's Visit

Here it was August 1941, and we were edging closer
and closer to the horrible devastation of a mighty world
war that would forever change our country and the lives of
our friends and neighbors. Still there was a general feeling
that President Roosevelt really meant it when he said we
would not get involved. It was summer time and my
friends and I thought of beach fun and boys. But there
was a mini-war brewing on the home front.

Every year tension crept into family life when Aunt
Goldie and Uncle Seymore went on vacation. Weeks
before, the unspoken question was, "Who will take Bubbie
for two weeks?" She was too old to stay alone.

I came up from my friend's apartment one Sunday and
wondered what all the noise was on the lower landings of
the stairway. Peering down, I saw two men struggling to
carry someone heavy. I could hear their voices, "Slow
down! My arms are breaking and we have another flight of
steps to go."

"I am going slow, Marvin. Any slower and I could sit
down and take a snooze.

"Enough with the smart talk, Seymore. Mama is
heavier than she looks. God forbid we should drop her."

"Listen, Marvin, don't even think such a thought. We
have enough trouble getting her up one flight without a
disaster on our hands."

I danced down the steps to greet my uncles. "How
wonderful! You brought Bubbie to our house. I thought
she was going to Connecticut to stay with Aunt Alice."

Uncle Marvin grunted as he helped lift Bubbie up
another step. "It would take the Eleventh Commandment
from God to make Alice give up her precious time to take

her mother. Two weeks--you'd think we were asking for a major sacrifice."

Bubbie's sweet voice interrupted the flow of complaints, "Sha, sha. Hello, sweetheart."

"Bubbie, I'm so glad you're staying with us. We'll have so much fun."

Uncle Seymore muttered, "Yeah, but your father wouldn't agree with you."

I didn't like it when anyone criticized Daddy, but I had to admit the truth. Daddy always fussed and fussed about Bubbie coming to stay at our house. "Why us?" he asked Mama. "We have no spare bedroom. I will have to sleep on the couch."

"Bubbie can sleep on a cot in the living room."

"Don't be ridiculous. She's an old woman."

"That's true." Mama usually got her way. I wondered if Daddy knew he had just lost.

This day Uncle Marvin and Uncle Seymore, their arms crossed fireman-carry style, answered my question as they deposited Bubbie at our door, "Of course we'll stay for lunch. Such a schlep back to Brooklyn."

Mama greeted Bubbie with a hug, got her settled in the kitchen, then bustled around setting the table for lunch. She interrupted her conversation in Yiddish to give me a nudge. "Wake up. Put out the rye bread and the herring from the ice box."

My uncles decided they would take a nap after lunch before starting the long trip back to Brooklyn from the Bronx. While my uncles slept, Mama said, "You will have to help me with Bubbie, my daughter. I am depending on you to keep her company." Mama wasn't asking. She was telling.

For the first time I understood Daddy's side of the argument. Though we both loved Bubbie, her visit made me give up my precious time and Daddy his precious privacy. I decided to become Daddy's ally.

The next evening Daddy and I were alone in the living room. Mama was helping Bubbie with a cooling bath before our Shabbos dinner. "How's business, Daddy?" I asked.

He raised his eyebrows. "Since when do you worry about the business?" His warm dark eyes paid careful attention to my expression, which I tried to keep innocent of my plan to undermine Mama.

"The other day you told Mama that your saleslady, Molly, was leaving on a two week vacation. I just wondered if I could earn a little money by taking her place after school."

"You mean you want to 'nosh' down my candy inventory? Last time you helped I think I lost money. Come on, tell me what's going on in that busy brain of yours." He ruffled my bangs, something that usually annoyed me, but today I tolerated his affectionate gesture.

I was too old to sit on his lap, but I leaned toward him and whispered, "Mama wants me to help with Bubbie."

"So, what's so terrible about that? You're crazy about Bubbie."

"Of course I am. But Mama listened to Aunt Alice when she called today. I know that Aunt Alice told her that I should help take the burden off Mama every day. She always tells me that."

Daddy's frown of annoyance was exactly what I expected. "Aunt Alice, huh? That woman gives advice about everything, but ask her to do her share and she disappears."

I kept quiet. Daddy didn't need any help to express his feelings about Mama's favorite sister. He continued, "Later she'll call and ask your mother to come to her house when her husband goes away on business. And your mother always goes."

This time I joined in his complaint to show my sympathy. "Yeah, and she always takes me. 'A nice country vacation' she tells me." Actually, I enjoyed staying at Aunt Alice's pretty house, but I left that out of the conversation.

Daddy looked at me with a little smile. "So you want to help your old Dad, huh?" His eyes signaled his enjoyment. "I can't pay you too much. And I'll only need you for those two weeks." I could tell by his smile that he understood the conspiracy.

"That's perfect! Bubbie leaves in two weeks." I blurted out. Embarrassed, I choked on my words but Daddy laughed.

"Tell you what. You can help me out three hours every other day, though I may only need you one hour. Would that be enough?" This time he actually winked. I had to resist winking back.

"Oh, yes! Daddy, you're so good to me." That would give me two hours to do as I pleased, not enough for the movies but enough time for my friends or to read the book I had taken out of the library.

Before dinner I retreated to my bedroom to leave Mama and Daddy alone in the living room. I didn't want to face Mama when Daddy told her of his plan to use me in his pharmacy. Mama sounded annoyed. I left my door open so I could hear them talking. "She's too young. She needs to relax."

I hardly breathed. Mama and Daddy held these talks only when we children were out of sight. But I was an expert at listening. That is how I discovered so many things they didn't want me to know. I could hear dishes clinking and Bubbie's slow movements in the kitchen. She was setting the table for our Shabbos dinner, *my* usual job. I had a twinge of guilt and was about to go help her when I heard Mama's voice again.

"By the way, your brother called today. He and Ruby are going to Paris for a week." Something in her voice made me let out my breath with a big whoosh. I couldn't see Mama, but I could tell she was finding a way for Daddy to change his mind about using me in the pharmacy.

"Bernard? Why didn't he call me at the store?"

"It seems he wanted to talk to me first. He would like me and the children--and you if possible--to stay at their house to take phone messages from his patients."

There was a long pause. "When are they leaving?"

"At the end of the month."

Another silence. Then, "Well, I guess I can commute to Brooklyn for a week. That way we can all be together."

"Yes, and the children will be finished with school. I don't mind giving Bernard a hand. After all, it's family."

There it was. The magic word. Mama helps Uncle Bernard. I help with Bubbie. No more discussion.

I almost felt sorry for Daddy. I walked into the living room and caught his eye. I knew it was over when he said

to Mama, "Perhaps Carole can help me later in the summer.
After all, Bubbie is here and she loves to be with Carole."

Mama adjusted her apron, nodded once, glanced at me
and said, "Of course and Carole loves to be with her
Bubbie." It was true, so why did guilt pinch away at my
flushed face?

I consoled myself by thinking that watching Bubbie
place a clean white kerchief over her head just before she
touched a match to the Shabbos candles was almost as
satisfying as being with my friends. I could read my book
with my flashlight under the covers at night; it was my
secret time to read.

I loved to see Bubbie wave her graceful fingers over
the tiny flames, then cover her eyes. She always wore her
prettiest silk dress, but on her fingers there would be only
one piece of jewelry: her gold wedding ring.

She would chant the blessings over the lights softly as
we all murmured the Hebrew words:
Baruch Atah Adenoy
Eloheinu melech ho'alom
Asher kid'shanu, b'mitzvotav
V'tzivanu, l'hadlik ner
Shel Shabbot.
"Omen," she'd whisper.
"Omen," we'd echo.

Daddy touched my arm, smiled and shrugged. Mama's
eyes were on Bubbie, but we knew she had won--again.

1942   The Neighborhood Will Talk

I was growing up very fast the second year of World
War II.

Bernice and I talked all the time about the long list of
the local boys who were serving in the military.
Sometimes, it felt good to forget the screaming headlines
and the constant talk on the radio about battles and
bombings. We even enjoyed returning to our childhood
and playing silly games we had played as kids in
elementary school. But because we were all too aware of

the boys in the neighborhood, we made subtle changes in our games. That wasn't always such a good idea.

Mama glanced sideways at me one afternoon and the little frown between her brows increased my anxiety. I needed to know what was behind Mama's opening comment, "A neighbor saw you yesterday." My mind did a fast run-through of Sunday's activities. I remembered walking to Woolworth's for a new lipstick and hanging around the corner candy store, hoping that Danny, the cute boy I met in my history class at high school, would come by. Then I went home. Wait a minute, I thought. Yes, yesterday a gang of the neighborhood kids had played Hide and Seek. Bingo!

"Mama, I think I had better start my homework."

"Just a minute, Carole," she said, drying her hands on the dishtowel she kept nearby. "Sit down at the table so we can talk."

I sat down, but my interest in cookies had strangely disappeared. Something told me I was going to hear an unpleasant story. Mama taking time to sit and drink coffee at four o'clock on a Monday afternoon confirmed my suspicions. One look at the wash told me that she had at least an hour of scrubbing before dinner.

She cleared her throat after sipping some of the steaming hot coffee-flavored milk. Very deliberately, she set her cup down and said, "A neighbor saw you in the cellar yesterday."

I swallowed hard, looked at Mama's closed face and answered, "Really? So what? You gave me stuff to put in the garbage cans."

She sipped again and said, "No, it was late in the day. You weren't alone."

"Who is this nosy woman? Why was she watching the cellar?"

Mama shook the crumbs from her apron into her hand and deposited them in her cup. Every motion seemed to slow down the way it did in those funny movie cameras I played with at Coney Island. Only my heart wouldn't slow down. It raced and galloped until I was sure Mama could hear the wild noise.

"It doesn't matter who she is. .She also said that it wasn't the first time she had seen you in the cellar with a boy.

There it was, a "boy". I started to speak, all the while watching Mama's hand around the coffee cup. When I pushed her to the limits of patience, she had on occasion used her hands to slap me into obedience. "Well, we hide sometimes in the cellar when we play games. It's cold outside and it's not such a terrible thing to do. I don't remember whether it was Anita or Betty with me or whoever." I hoped to move her away from the dangerous word.

Mama shook her head, "Not Anita, not Betty, my daughter. She said a boy."

"Maybe it was, but we all play Hide and Seek together. It's not so terrible to hide in the cellar with a boy."

The word hung in the air between us. My stomach turned. I knew what "boy" rhymed with, but I didn't want Mama to follow my thoughts.

Mama followed her own path to this inquisition. "The neighbors will talk. Nice girls don't go in the cellar with boys. A nice Jewish girl doesn't go in the cellar with a goy."

As usual, Mama didn't need a map to know my mind. I tried whining, "It was so cold outside, and I didn't want to be alone in the cellar. I asked Joe to come in there with me because the janitor sometimes looks at me funny."

The name slipped out in my nervousness. Mama's hand was on my arm, tight and hard. "Joe? That Italian boy with the skinny face? He's older than you are, but he goes to the same grade you do. Are you meshuga? Bad enough he's not Jewish. He's not smart, either."

Mama always told me to choose smart friends. "People will judge you by who they see you with," she'd say.

I hurried on, "Oh, Mama, you are *so* prejudiced! We are only kids. I don't think about who is Jewish or who is smart."

She tightened her hold on my hand and said, "Then think about what could happen to you in the cellar. Girls can get in trouble in dark places with older boys."

I understood what Mama meant. When she combined "girls" and "trouble," she meant having a baby. Mama never told me how girls have babies; I learned *that* from my friends. It took me months before I could accept the fact that my mother and my father had produced Michael and me by doing what my friends told me.

"God, Mama, we only kissed a little! All the guys and girls do that."

Her eyes glittered at me through her glasses. "You were alone with that boy a long time. What did you do after the kisses?"

That upset me. "What do you think I am? One of those bad girls? We just kissed and then ran out when we heard footsteps coming."

Mama only stared at me as if she could assure herself that I was telling the truth by examining my face. "You are not to go into a cellar with a boy--not even a *Jewish* boy. Your father will have to be told."

I was worried about Daddy. Mama usually hinted at the dangers of growing up around boys, but Daddy tried to put the fear of the Devil in my heart. He always questioned me about my friends and warned me to be careful. His word "careful" meant the same thing as Mama's "trouble."

Daddy made a point of telling me stories about girls who came into his pharmacy and said, "Doc, give me something to get rid of this baby, I'm pregnant." He watched me as if I were a fragile little flower that everyone wanted to pick. I had to be home every night at nine thirty on summer evenings when kids loved to stay up late to joke and sing popular songs. If I were late, he'd come looking for me with a stormy face.

I sometimes asked my best friend, "What do men and women do that's so bad? Why do our Dads worry about us so much?"

She'd sigh and admit that her Dad was just as awful as mine. Then we wished we could grow up a lot faster.

That night after dinner, Daddy told me he wanted to talk to me. Daddy's corner of the living room was always messy with his magazines and newspapers tossed all over the footrest as well as on the floor. He took his time, puffed on his cigarette and concentrated on the glowing ash at the tip. I stared at it too, taken by the deepening of the color as Daddy pulled in on his breath. It was nice to share a peaceful moment.

But a moment it was. "Your mother told me that you were seen kissing a boy in the cellar." Daddy always came directly to the problem at hand, unlike Mama who played with it like a cat plays with a mouse.

I tried to be even more direct. "Mama and I had a good talk, and I agreed not to go into the cellar with a boy any more." I prayed that I had deflected some of the storm by admitting my error, although I certainly didn't see what the whole fuss was about. Kissing was more fun than running around searching for the hiding places of the other kids.

"Mama worries about you very much. She remembers girls in Russia who became pregnant from village brutes or from the soldiers who rode into town, drinking and wearing their uniforms that the girls loved."

"I never heard that story before. Mama was so young when she left for America. How could she remember that?"

My father's lips twitched. He answered, "Your mother has five sisters, two of whom took every opportunity to fill your mother's head with horror stories. You are so lucky to have parents who care a great deal. We don't want you to suffer or to get into trouble."

Daddy started a long lecture on biology, what we kids called the "birds and the bees" story. I listened politely, then came to startled attention. He had just said that foolish boys and girls didn't use "protection". My face flushed. Did Daddy know that I had found that rolled up piece of rubber in his drawer where Mama put his socks? I had helped Mama with the laundry, but I didn't tell her what I had seen. She'd tell me not to look! I decided not to interrupt Daddy. To protect myself in a different way, I let my mind float around to the movie stars I adored and to the pretty red dress I had seen in a department store. Suddenly, I thought of Joe's kisses and heaved a huge sigh, earning myself a disgusted look from Daddy. "Young lady, I doubt that you heard one word I said. Your mother was right. You don't keep your mind on what is important for very long. I thought I could appeal to your intellect, but I see that I was wrong."

I smiled as sweetly as I could. Usually that worked with Daddy though rarely with Mama who knew me too well. When she was in a particularly good mood, she said I reminded her of herself when she was a young girl. Maybe when I see her in that mood, I thought, I could get her to tell me all those stories about the girls in Russia. Soldiers, how romantic...

Daddy put his hand on my head and said, "All right. You can do your homework now. One thing I want you to remember... boys will be boys, whether they're Jewish or not. I won't have my daughter get into trouble like those poor girls who come begging me to help them. No more cellars. I wish I could say, 'no more boys', too," he sighed.

After that, Mama tried to keep me very busy. I could feel her eyes on me when I told her I was meeting my friends, but she did not say a word. Daddy continued to lecture whenever I came home a few minutes late. When warm weather finally came, we kids went to nearby Bronx Park and played our games there. We kissed and hugged and felt very grown up.

What Mama didn't realize was that she had done such a good job of instilling virtue in me that I would never even *think* about getting into trouble--the word she feared so much. Innocent dreams of handsome soldiers in uniform were as far as I went.

Years later, Mama confessed that it was *she* who had seen me kissing my friend Joe in the dirty cellar. I also found out that Joe, the Italian boy who had kissed so sweetly, died in the cold, white snow during the Battle of the Bulge where he wore the uniform of the troops who fought on skis. Mama cried when I told her.

1946   A Cousin's Pain

The war was finally over. Michael came home from service, and Mama began to smile again. A neighbor on the same floor rarely smiled. Her son had been killed in a ghastly accident: beheaded by airplane propellers when he came too close to inspect the engines. How could that woman live? I wondered. She was so brave, saying hello to me when we met on the steps.

We discovered that some wartime experiences may not have killed but damaged some soldiers terribly.

"Saul is coming to visit," Mama announced after a short phone call.

"That's unusual," Daddy said, "I can't remember the last time your brother came back to New York."

I heard part of their conversation, but I was mostly deep into "Studs Lonigan", a dirty book my brother Michael bought from a friend. Every guy in the neighborhood had borrowed it from Michael, but finally he said I could read it if I served him water at dinner every day for a year. "When are you going to grow up?" I asked him. "You're back from the war, but you're still acting like we were little kids."

When Mama added that Uncle Saul was bringing my cousin Abe with him, I put my finger in the book to mark my place. I remembered that I had a crush on Abe when I saw him a year or so before the war began. I wondered if he was still so quiet and cute-looking. "Did Uncle Saul say why Abe was coming, too?" I asked.

Mama frowned. "Not so I could understand. He sounded so upset. My brother doesn't like to worry the family, but he said Abe was in some kind of trouble." She turned to Michael, "Your uncle particularly wanted you to talk to Abe."

Michael stretched his long legs out on the couch. Only he could get away with putting his shoes up on the furniture. I watched the trembling ash of his cigarette, almost hoping it would fall. He'd catch it from Mama if he burned a hole in the couch cover. He couldn't remain a war hero forever, even in Mama's eyes. After all he had only been in the army a year and a half, a lot less than some of the guys I knew.

He yawned, put down the paper and said, "Don't know how I can help him, but it might be fun to swap war stories." I knew without looking at her that Mama was smiling at Michael. Daddy spoke up from behind his section of the *New York Times*, "Is he able to work since he came home?"

I noticed Mama's warning look and wondered what was going on. I was used to her secrets, but this one interested me enough to make me close my book. "Why wouldn't he be able to work? Are there fewer jobs in Philadelphia?" I asked Michael.

"Beats me. We'll probably find out when they get here. Are you still fluttering over Abe, little sister? Don't you know that cousins shouldn't marry?"

I was tempted to pitch the book at him, but was held back by Mama's suspicious look. I could hear her saying, "In this house we don't throw things."

Michael wagged his finger at me and said, "No, no, little sister. That's *my* book you're thinking of throwing. Your aim probably hasn't improved since the last time you tried it."

Mama's distracted voice brought the two of us back to Uncle Saul. "I'm going to call my sister Goldie and find out if she knows why Saul is coming. He just said that we should come to Goldie's house tomorrow."

"Too bad he's coming on a Sunday; I'm keeping the drug store open every weekend now." Daddy didn't sound the least bit sorry that he wouldn't be able to go. Family conferences bored him.

"Michael will drive us. I'll call Goldie now."

On Sunday, Michael and I helped Mama carry the packages to the car. With Michael's new car, it was easy to bring all the cakes and cookies that Mama took to family gatherings, as if there weren't wonderful Jewish bakeries in Brooklyn. What a pleasure it was to avoid the creaky old trains that we used to take to see Bubbie and Aunt Goldie.

Michael whistled through his teeth while he drove, Mama sat next to him with her eyes closed, and I stared out the window at the view of the Hudson River and the Palisades. I loved the sight of the busy George Washington Bridge on our left and the overwhelming New York skyscrapers, so impressive even from a distance.

I remembered the last time I saw Abe. His brown hair hung over his forehead, almost hiding those interesting tip-tilted eyes.

"Do you remember how Abe disliked big parties?" I asked Michael. He nodded and wondered if the war had changed Abe. I said, " I don't know, but Mama sure has calmed down since you came home. Every time she worried about you, she baked up a storm, and I gained ten pounds eating the results!"

Michael grinned, but I was happy he couldn't see me. I noshed from the bags of cookies. When we passed Prospect Park and arrived at Aunt Goldie's house, I headed straight for the kitchen, so clean and inviting, with all the great smells of cooking from the old pots on the stove. Instead of her usual smile and hug, Aunt Goldie said, "Shh, find a chair behind the grownups, darling."

The family always gathered in Aunt Goldie's kitchen for important talks. Usually, it was hard to hear anyone speak, so noisy was the gossiping that went on around the old oak table that Bubbie bought for their first house when they arrived from Russia. What stories that table heard about weddings, bar mitzvahs, and sorrowful accounts of old friends who had died. Mama and Michael sat at the table with Aunt Goldie, Uncle Saul, and my cousin Abe. What surprised me most was that Aunt Alice had come in from her home in Connecticut for this family discussion. As always, Aunt Alice dressed in bright clothes that were more suitable for me than for her, but I envied the confident way she sat with her legs crossed, her long red nails tapping an impatient message on the table. I kissed my uncle, and said a shy "Hello" to Abe, who nodded and quickly looked away.

Mama sat with her back straight against the kitchen chair. "So," she said, her eyes peering kindly at my cousin, "what is so important that you had to shlep us all the way to Brooklyn?" Her words made the question seem light, but I could sense the strain behind the words. Mama was worried and I couldn't figure out why.

Uncle Saul glanced quickly at Abe, who was holding his hands tightly around his body. Then my uncle puffed out his lips, let the air out with a long, sighing sound and spoke. "Well, Marsha dear, Abe has been very nervous since he came home from the army. He needs to go out and find himself a position in a drug store, but now he says he can't even look for work."

Mama and Aunt Alice moved closer to Abe, but it was Aunt Alice, as the oldest sister in the family, who spoke first. "Abe, darling," she said, "your father loves you very much. Think of all the trouble he went to, driving all the way to Brooklyn to see the family. What can we do to help you? Is it money? I'll give you a loan. Maybe you want to go into business for yourself."

Abe's hands were like two helpless birds, as they lifted into the air, fluttered there and then settled down again, finally resting on his knees. While we waited for him to speak, the tension grew. Everyone could see that Abe's problem had nothing to do with money. He cleared his throat, spoke too softly to be heard, then tried again. "No one can help. I have no desire to get up in the morning. I don't want to eat. I can't think about the future. All I know is that I hurt." He stopped to sip a glass of water that Aunt Goldie placed before him.

Mama asked Aunt Alice to change seats with her. She placed one hand over Abe's fingers that still moved restlessly on his lap. While she spoke, she kept her long, graceful fingers laced through Abe's and held them still. "The future will happen anyhow, whether you think about it or not. Meanwhile, your parents are in terrible pain."

Abe struggled to pull his hands out from under Mama's. He stood up suddenly and leaned over to stare into her eyes. "What do they know about pain? What do they know about going to war whole and coming home with parts of yourself gone forever?" He walked with a stumbling, uneven gait, holding on tightly to the table. "Look at me. Why should I get out of bed when I can hardly walk?"

He pulled up the pant leg nearest to Mama and said, "That thing attached to my knee is supposed to take the place of my foot, but my foot is gone. Sometimes I wake up and the foot that isn't there hurts so much that I cry out."

Uncle Saul covered his face with his hands as Abe talked. "Pain, that's pain. What do my parents or any of you know about pain?" He fell back into his chair, and for a few minutes no one spoke. Mama moved her hands gently over his leg, stroking and stroking it as if to take away all the hurt.

I couldn't control the tears that started the minute Abe tried to walk. Why hadn't Mama told me about Abe's war wounds? I could feel her eyes on me, and when I could face her without crying, I saw that she too, struggled with tears. She shook her head at me and signaled to Michael to comfort me. Michael put his arm around my shoulder, but directed his words to Abe. My fun-loving brother spoke so seriously that I realized that I had never heard that tone in his voice before.

"What you are suffering from I can understand. I'm lucky I came home in one piece. Do you still hear the big guns when you try to sleep at night? I know I do. Do you hear the moans of soldiers who have been terribly hurt? I do." He stopped and shook his head from side to side. "No one comes home from war whole. Even those who didn't lose arms and legs are changed forever. There are thousands of us who understand your pain, Abe."

Mama's pride in Michael made her face pink and young. I stared at her, hungrily wishing that I could make her look like that, too. Without thinking, I stood up, walked over to Abe, and took his trembling hand in mine. "I was just a scared kid during the war. I saw my mother grow thin and pale every time the mailman had no mail from Michael, who was overseas. Mama and Daddy listened to every bit of news about the war, and they suffered so much when we heard about the awful Battle of the Bulge. I hardly know you, Abe, but you made me care."

Abe squeezed my hand. I realized that whatever had happened to him hadn't stolen his young strength. I smiled and said, "Ouch! What a grip you have." He grinned back at me, and everyone sighed deeply and relaxed.

Mama also smiled and I knew that I had pleased her. Abe and Michael sat down in the living room. I could hear Michael say, "Why don't you come down to the store where I work. It's very busy and can give you an idea of what a typical day would be like in almost any city drug store." Abe looked almost as young as the boy I remembered, his eyes alert and his hands rested peacefully on the leg that Mama had stroked. I touched Mama's arm. "Why didn't you tell me what happened to Abe?"

Mama hugged me hard against her body and smoothed down my unruly hair. "My darling daughter, I didn't want you to hurt for your cousin. What good would it do anything if you knew? My sisters and I cried enough for the whole family. Today your tears came from the heart. You saw your cousin hurting, and you cried, but what sweet thoughts you expressed. You made Abe feel better, and you made me very proud."

Mama's words created a lovely floating feeling inside my head. For the rest of the afternoon, I walked around with a silly grin on my face. Michael watched me wolf down two helpings of Aunt Goldie's meatloaf and whispered, "Take it easy, kid. That stuff goes down like a lead balloon. I don't want the back of my car to scrap along the road on the way home."

I wrinkled my nose at Michael, but for the first time I didn't argue or even act annoyed. Instead I said, "You were wonderful the way you talked to Abe. I got goose bumps listening to you. You helped me to understand why Uncle Saul called the family together."

"Yeah," Michael said, "Mama always claimed that when there's trouble in a family, everyone should share it."

I felt so grown up and delighted that Michael and I could talk and not act in our old silly way. I even had the confidence to sit down next to Abe when we all ate dinner. He smiled at me in a new way that made me blush and stammer a bit as we talked. I liked his smile when he looked at me. If he was still in pain, he didn't show it.

1947   Mama's First Admirer

I had my own warrior from the war. I met Jack, who had been a navigator of a B17, and was trying hard to return to civilian life when we met. Life was so sweet; I had graduated from Hunter College, fallen madly in love, and had agreed to marry my sweetheart after he finished his graduate work in 1948 in Berkeley, California. Just as Mama had lived for Michael's letters during the war, I lived for Jack's letters.

Mama never indulged in "girl" talk with me, except for one desperate moment when I opened a letter from Jack early in our long-distance romance. Mama was scrubbing clothes on her washboard in the kitchen while I quickly scanned the letter from far away California.

When I threw the letter down and burst into tears, Mama hurried over to me without even wiping her hands. I felt the hot, sudsy water soaking into my blouse as she pulled me into her arms, but nothing mattered except my careening emotions. I pushed Mama away and stared out the kitchen window at the faded red brick wall across the way from our apartment.

"What has happened? Is Jack sick or hurt, God forbid?" Mama sat down next to me at the old kitchen table.

I gulped down the sour-tasting tears and reached out to crush Jack's letter between my fingers, but Mama took the letter from me and read it slowly. It didn't surprise me that she read my mail. Mama never expected us to keep secrets from her, although she routinely kept secrets from us. Besides, I was used to sharing parts of Jack's letters with her. She enjoyed hearing about California, despite her worries that I would live there with Jack after we married. "At least he went to California to study," she said, but I suffered the long months of separation.

I didn't wait for Mama to finish reading. "We are engaged to be married, and suddenly he wants time to think about our relationship. I hate him! There must be another girl in his life." My tears flowed freely again until Mama found her handkerchief and wiped my wet face.

"So what makes you so smart that you can see across three thousand miles? I didn't read a word about a girl. Did you get other letters this week?"

I chewed my lip and nodded, "Yes but they were short, and in one he forgot to end with 'I love you' the way he always does."

"Maybe he had a test or something else on his mind. Is there anything else he sounded worried about?" Mama's voice turned dry and practical, as if she were asking me about his eating habits.

"All he says is that this isn't a good time for us to marry. He's used up most of the money he saved when he was in the Air Force. I guess he's not sure if he can afford a wife."

Anger was taking the edge off my pain. "My life isn't so great, either. I can't go out on dates the way my friends do. Not that I want to...." I hurried to say, pushing down the guilty thoughts that denied my last words. I was in my junior year of college, enjoying the other guys that I met, though I never accepted their requests for dates. "He has females all around him, probably gorgeous California blondes with long legs. All I do is go to the movies with his sisters on weekends. I feel chaperoned. It's not fair."

I could see Mama's lips twitching in silent amusement, but she maintained her casual tone. "Perhaps Jack is thinking about you and feeling bad that you aren't going out more. After all, he's older than you are. Maybe a little wiser, too. What do you think?"

Mama made me feel young and foolish. More than a little miffed, I snapped, "I think he's having second thoughts about loving me. But then, your experience is limited to Daddy. I can't expect you to understand."

Mama didn't answer. She just looked down at her fingers and twisted her plain gold wedding band. Finally she said, "Don't be so quick to talk about what you don't know. I wasn't always just a housewife and your Mama." She stood up, kissed the top of my head, and went back to her scrub board. "I need to finish a few more shirts. Then it will be time to put dinner on the stove. Set the table, Carole. It will take your mind off your trouble."

I moved around the table with the silverware and dishes, all the time wondering what Mama was hiding. "Will you talk to me after dinner?"

She turned and smiled. "Yes, my daughter, if you help me clean up the kitchen." Usually I balked and tried to find excuses to get out of this extra chore. Every Friday I found new reasons why I needed the time to do school work or to make an important phone call. After all, I had already helped by dusting the furniture and sifting the flour for the apple pie she always made on Shabbos. This evening I only nodded and brooded about the question Jack's letter had left in my mind: was I really ready to marry?

After dinner, Michael and Daddy went into the living room and lost themselves in their cigarettes and newspapers. As always, Mama muttered in Yiddish and English about their "filthy" habit. All I heard was, "Vey is meir. My clean house. Their shmutzike cigarettes!"

I stayed in the kitchen, cleared the table and dried the dishes while Mama washed and kept her thoughts to herself. When we finished cleaning, Mama took off her pretty, rose-strewn apron and sat down at the table.

She reached for the huge family album that she liked to keep in the kitchen to look at when she took time to rest. I, too, loved to pore over the photos, marveling at the young faces of the family, especially Mama who wore her hair soft and straight with one strand slipping out to hide her eyes. She looked even younger without the glasses.

I peeked over Mama's shoulder as she turned the pages. We both laughed at the pictures of Daddy in the bathing suit with the dark, sleeveless top and at the pictures of Michael and me when we were little. The photos made me think of us as cute kids who somehow weren't really us.

Mama pulled the album closer, adjusted her glasses, and turned to a page close to the beginning of the book. I knew that page by heart; all the pictures were of my aunts and uncles and some of their friends and cousins.

Mama's fingers went to a familiar picture of herself and a cousin who had his arms around her. I had seen the picture so often that I felt as if I knew this man, but Mama startled me by saying, "This is the cousin I almost married."

"You never told me that before. What was he like? What happened to him? Did you know Daddy yet?" The questions tumbled out, but I instinctively lowered my voice so that Daddy couldn't hear us.

Mama, too, spoke in hushed tones. She took off her glasses, pushed her hair down on her forehead and asked, "Do I look like her any more?" How odd. She spoke of herself in the third person. Yet, surely it wasn't that odd because the young woman in the picture wasn't Mama to me, either. This woman wore a long white, starched dress with a lovely, capelike collar and a flaring tiered skirt that flowed from a tight, trim waist band. Her hair, parted in the center, rested in two deep waves over her forehead, then dropped straight down in a short bob.

"His name was Daniel. He lived with his mother, Bubbie's sister, only a block away from our house. I don't know where he is today, married I suppose, but not in New York."

"Did you love him, Mama? I caught my breath after I asked the question. What a traitor I was to Daddy even having the thought.

Mama stared at the picture and said, "He was family. I thought I loved him. He could remember things about our village in Russia, which I had forgotten except when my sisters told me stories about my childhood. Best of all, Daniel remembered my Papa. 'He was so good', he'd tell me. 'No one in the village was surprised when he died young. He worked long hours to make a living in his tiny tailor shop, but then I'd always see him after hours reading the Talmud, nodding his head and staring up at the sky. When I talked to him, he'd hug me or give me a piece of fruit he'd find in his jacket pocket.'"

Mama sighed happily as she thought as always about her beloved Papa. "Did you and Daniel talk of marriage?" I asked.

"Yes," Mama said, a frown replacing the smile. "My sisters all told me to marry Daniel, that he would fit in perfectly with our family. Even Bubbie pushed me to marry. But something was missing. When I saw pictures of the two of us, I felt strange. He looked so much like my brothers, who also urged me to marry him."

"What was missing?" I wanted her to remain in the past, so I could learn more about this sweet-faced woman who became my Mama years later.

Mama shrugged, almost impatiently. "There was no mystery. I knew exactly what shirt he would wear with which suit, I knew his favorite foods, and I always knew he'd bring me a bunch of yellow daisies when he came to call. I didn't want him to kiss me, but I let him. He was a nice man. How could I hurt his feelings?"

Mama tapped her long fingers on the frayed album cover. "One day I locked myself in my bedroom and wouldn't come out or answer anyone's questions."

I hugged my knees in excitement, Jack's letter forgotten. "Why, Mama, why?"

"My brothers had told me the night before that they all wanted me to tell Daniel I'd marry him soon. They were angry, saying poor Daniel, he looked so upset whenever he left our house. I went to bed that night, feeling sick and separated from the family for the first time that I could remember."

"I'm glad you didn't marry Daniel," I said. Mama smiled and hugged me the way she had when I was a little girl listening to her stories.

"I met your Daddy soon after that. He worked part-time in the corner drug store and would always talk to me in a friendly way. I liked his dark eyes and his wavy hair, but, most of all, I liked the shy way he'd look at me. One day he asked me to go to a concert in the park that night."

"How romantic," I breathed, turning to pictures of Daddy, trim and serious with brown eyes. Mama traced his strongly curved lips idly while we sat closely together.

"Yes. He brought me a red rose--just one, and began to court me openly after that night. At first the family hardly spoke to him, but I refused to let them persuade me to see Daniel when he came to call. After a while, he understood and only visited the family when he knew I was away."

"How did you know you loved Daddy?" I waited anxiously for her answer. Jack's letter popped up again in my mind, and pain and confusion returned in full force.

Mama straightened her back. She said, "I wanted
to be with him all the time. I'd walk past the drug store
and watch him when he didn't know I was there. I did that
many times during our life together. He brought me books
to read and talked about ideas that only my Papa had ever
mentioned to me." She paused, and a pink flush suffused
her creamy-white skin, "He kissed me and I didn't want
him to stop. Think about your feelings, my daughter. Let
Jack know that you are ready to marry. Perhaps he needs
you to tell him that."

Mama took my face in her hands, kissed me
tenderly on the cheek, and said, "Marriage is a big step. If
you are sure, be the strong one and help him find the
courage. Sometimes it takes a woman to see into the
future."

I sat dreaming in the kitchen when Mama left to join
Daddy in the living room. "I made some tea, dear," she
said. "Would you like a cup?" I didn't hear his answer,
but somehow I knew they had once again expressed their
love.

LETTERS FROM THE HEART
THE FAMILY

Mama wrote to Uncle Saul asking for help in applying for citizenship. His response gave her the information she needed:
(Uncle Saul's English was not always correct.)

Dear Mary,

   I received your letter and was very glad to hear from you all. I want to write you again about your entry into this country in the year 1911, the month August 29 on the ship Waterland, the port Bremen. Your name Mary or Marsha, first name does not make much different. But your second name was Abramowiez. You came from Horadisht, state of Minsk from Russia and the rest wouldn't make any different now.

I wish you luck.

Your brother,

Saul

Darling Mama,

  The thing I desire most is to lay the world at your feet some day. Only God knows how much your family loves you and how much they want to give you. In our hearts, you come before us, because we believe you are the most wonderful mother, wife, and woman in the world. I love you so much it hurts. (Except when I have to do the dishes!) Until we can lay the world at your feet, we can at least keep them warm. Lots of love and a Happy Birthday. We hope the slippers fit.

Lovingly,

Carole and Michael

  (I had to add Michael's name to the letter because he supplied the money to buy the red wool slippers.)

Mama's greatest pleasure was to give me gifts that were important to both of us. She gave me a music box from Paris that I cherish to this day. With her gift, came this letter:

Darling,

It's the song I heard in my childhood. It's the song I will never forget. It's the song my dear mother sang in my dreams. I can hear her yet. "Go to sleep my baby, my baby once more on my knee." Of all the songs I ever heard, that's the song of songs for me. It's something beautiful to remember and it's true.

Here's the music box that you loved in your childhood. That too, my daughter, you'll never forget as you loved it and had to play it all the time. I, too, played it often and you were near me. I cherished it all these years. This is my gift of love for you, and may there be a song of love and happiness for you too, my child to remember.

With all my love,

Your Mother

For 17 years after my husband and I moved to California, I wrote and wrote--for a short time, every day, and then every week:

Dearest Mama,   Oct. 1948

    We have been on the road for almost three days and every day I go to bed weary but full of the wonderful sights we have seen. I am so lucky to be with my husband, sharing the glorious changes of the color in October, far more beautiful than anything we saw in New York. I wish I could share them with you, but we took lots of pictures and at least you will see those. Too bad they're not in color, but we can't afford that. Most of all, I want you to know that I fall asleep thinking of you and Daddy every night. Please don't worry. We are very careful about what we eat and how we drive. I know you asked us to call home every night until we reach Berkeley, but we are so tired from the long hours on the road that I can call every other day. I have sent a card or letter every day, so you should soon begin to receive a few of them. I love you very much and I am so excited about my new life.

Kisses to you and Daddy,

Your daughter

Over the years Daddy wrote infrequently, so each letter became very important to me. I'm glad I kept the one he wrote when we finally arrived in Berkeley after our long drive across country. It came right after Truman defeated Dewey:

My Dearest,   1948

I am very much relieved after having been waiting a week that you have at last reached your destination--and are well and happy--will write more in a day or two--as I am tired due to [listening to] the election returns.

Enclosed are certain papers from Hunter College, also a card from Columbia in reference to your Masters Degree. Of course, dear, we miss you very much!

With love to you both,

Your Pop

I wrote to Mama when I became pregnant with my first child. Only a year before Jack had lost his mother, and he was determined to bring another life into the world:

Dear Mama,   1952

    I'm glad we had a good talk on the phone last week. It's hard to believe I'm going to have a baby. Of course I want you with me, but I want you to decide whether you can come. It's expensive and I can't help you with that. I will understand no matter what you choose to do.
    Jack wants you too, believe me, Mama dear. He still misses his mother, but he values you very much. If you or Daddy are not well, don't even think of coming. I am a big girl now and know that there are things that you have to consider. I'm sure I'll have my baby safely and happily; hundreds of daughters do it every day. So do what is best for you to have peace of mind.

I love you,

Carole

I was grateful that Mama did come for the birth of our baby. In fact, she stayed with us for six weeks. When Mama had to leave, I kept her informed about her adorable grandson in every letter I wrote:

Dearest Mama,   1952

   You would have loved to see the baby in his tub today. He splashed and gasped when the water hit his face. Jack and I laughed at his startled expression. Don't worry, we take pictures of everything he does. But sometimes I cry because he's so beautiful, and I want to share him with you.

I love you,

Carole

Mama wrote back and both happiness and sadness came across in her words:

My darling daughter,

   Give my baby a kiss from his Nannie. At least I had the joy of seeing him when you brought him home from the hospital; you put him in my arms and said, "Here's your bundle of joy." When I held him, I thought he was my own baby. I miss him so much.

Love,

Mama

There were times when my letters over the years would be delayed, or I would be too busy to write. Mama's letters then would be painful to read, and I knew that I had hurt her deeply:

My darling daughter,

We haven't heard from you in almost two weeks. I worry so much. Are you sick? Did Jack have an accident? After all, he's only been driving for a year. Please do not try to get your driving license yet. Let Jack take you places.

Sometimes I ask God why he is punishing me that my child left me to go so far away. I must have done something wrong. Every day I look in the mail box, but there is not a letter from my daughter. I feel the sun has gone under a cloud. Please write my daughter, and tell me you are all right.

Your loving

Mama

Mama's complaints upset me, for they rarely changed. My
family responsibilities did, however. Our babies were born,
and I eventually went back to a teaching career.

Dear Mama,   1967

   What has God to do with my writing to you?
I feel terrible. Is that what you want me to feel? Try to
understand that I am very busy teaching and trying to do
everything to make home a pleasant place as well. After
all, you never had to work outside the home as I do. Now
don't get angry, after all you and Daddy always wanted me
to be a teacher, didn't you? I will try to write as often as I
can. You have to admit that most of the time I am very
good.

I love you,

Carole

Jack gave Mama a card on the first Mother's Day after our wedding. His message still touches me:

Dear Marsha,   1949

    No measure of thanks can ever indicate the extent to which I am indebted to you for the darling we both love; except the promise to cherish her with all my heart, and offer her the same strong love you have given her all her life.

Jack

Twenty years later Mama returned the same card to Jack with her own message added:

Darling Jack,

    I kept this card for 20 short years, and you kept your promise. May your love for one another continue the next 20 years and many more.

    Thank you so much.

Love,

Marsha

Michael and Daddy

1931 Aunt Nettie, Bubbie & Mama

1920 Mama

Jack & Carole

Carole

1945 Daddy at the Bronx elevated
train station

1937 Michael & Mama

Bubbie

Mama at the age of 16

1948 Jack & Carole's Wedding
Top: Aunt Alice, Aunt Goldie, Aunt Miriam, Aunt Nettie, Uncle Sam
Bottom: Aunt Hester, Bubbie, Carole, Jack, Mama, Daddy

Aunt Nettie, Uncle Seymore,
Aunt Goldie

Top: Mama, Aunt Miriam, Aunt Goldie
Bottom: Daddy, Aunt Nettie,
Uncle Marvin

1946 Aunt Nettie, Mama

Daddy

Uncle Harry

Uncle Bernard, Aunt Ruby

Uncle Seymore, Aunt Goldie

1969 Fred, Carole, Ron, Charles

Top: Uncle Marvin, Uncle Harry, Family Friend
Bottom: Aunt Nettie, Mama, Aunt Alice

Mama, Aunt Goldie, Aunt Nettie, Aunt Miriam,
Aunt Hester

Mama & early admirer

Château de Chillon et la Dent du Midi.

August /10/16.

Thou has taught me, Silent River.
Many a lesson deep and long;
Thou has been agenerous giver;
I can give thee but a sung.
Oft in sadness and in illness
I have watched thy current glide
Till the beauty of its stillness
Overflowed me, like a tide.
Jack.

Miss mary
Abrams.

Serie 79   3154

Daddy's card to Mama

Daddy in Prospect Park,
Brooklyn

Mama, Michael & Carole

Aunt Alice & Mama in
Waterbury, Conn.

Aunt Alice at Coney Island

Michael & Carole

Carole (6 months pregnant) with Jack in
Berkeley, CA

Stella & Carole

Aunt Goldie, Stella, Bubbie, Mama

BREAKING THE FAMILY HOLD

1948   Wedding Battle Lines

I awoke with the feeling that something was happening. I could see light filtering under the partially open bedroom door. Curious to discover who was up and around so early in the morning, I groped for the knob and peeked into Mama's room, just outside Michael's and mine. Daddy's body created a lump on his side of the bed, but Mama's side was vacant. Was she ill?

After pulling on a light robe, I tiptoed through the dim living room and connecting hallway, drawn to the kitchen light. There sat Mama drinking steaming milk, colored slightly with coffee, her favorite drink, and concentrating on the papers spread out on the red and white vinyl table cloth.

"What on earth is so important that it drags you out of bed before six o'clock in the morning?" I said, coming up behind her and looking over her shoulder.

"So I could ask you the same question--especially since you and Jack were out here till two in the morning." Jack and I, so soon to be married, figured there would be plenty of time to sleep after the wedding.

"We had to discuss our plans for California. You never like it when I talk about leaving, so we go over our list of things to do when we're alone."

Mama's lips tightened and her fingers clutched at the papers in front of her. "Yes, but you need to be resting for your wedding, not staying up half the night." Her voice quavered, and I resisted the urge to hug her. The tension between us in the weeks before the wedding had grown into smoldering resentment.

But my response was as matter of fact as I could make it. "Are those the invitation lists? " I knew exactly what she was doing, but I was trying to return to less emotional territory. Mama's pain and anger affected me deeply, but I would not beg her forgiveness for leaving her.

"Your mother-in-law invited so many extra people that I have a headache trying to make up the table seating arrangements."

I felt both annoyed and understanding of Mama's antagonism. She and I wandered like lost children in the world of marriage details. Now Mama and I were stuck with the problem of having to squeeze too many people into the wedding hall of the old synagogue where the marriage would take place.

"I told you I'd help you with the seating plans," I offered, trying once more to placate Mama. My desire to shout, "Damn it, Mama! I'm going to California, not to the moon so stop punishing me!" made me squirm around on the uncomfortable wooden chair. Instead I asked, "Why are you still fussing with the lists?"

"Because," she said, "I'm going to have to seat Uncle Bernard with Aunt Hester and her family." I let the silence grow between us. I could hear the little white clock on the refrigerator ticking away the minutes. I kept my eyes down, looking at my carefully polished nails.

Uncle Bernard was Daddy's older brother, the proud doctor whose very presence in a roomful of people made everyone sit up straighter. I loved him dearly for he had taken such tender care of me during my childhood bouts with pneumonia and assorted diseases.

And Mama intended to seat Uncle Bernard with Aunt Hester and her family? I opened my mouth, shut it and finally was able to say, "Let's rethink that, Mama. Uncle Bernard does not belong at the table with your sister and her family. You know that."

Mama faced me when I sat down next to her. The faint light of dawn came through the corner window, just enough so I could see the clothesline stretching out from the window to a pole in the center of the backyard. Somewhere out there, an unseen neighbor coughed and the garbage trucks broke the silence with their rumbling groans. Ordinarily, I enjoyed these early noises, so familiar to me from childhood on.

But Mama's voice, underscoring each word with firm resolve, deepened the tension between us. "This is the way I worked it out. This is the way it will have to be."

I gave up all pretense of reconciliation. "And what does Daddy think of this ridiculous idea?"

"Don't raise your voice to me. I will explain my reasons to your father. When you pay for the wedding, you can make the arrangements."

I started to protest even more, but held back my anger, responding to the years of training when Mama would say, "Never raise your voices to your parents, children." Michael and I rarely forgot that stern injunction.

I cornered my father after dinner when Mama went to ask a neighbor about flower arrangements. "Daddy, Mama wants to seat Uncle Bernard with Aunt Hester, Uncle Sherman, and their whole family. Please help me change her mind. You know that Aunt Hester will blow cigarette smoke in everyone's eyes and Uncle Sherman will tell dirty jokes. I'll just die of embarrassment."

Daddy shocked me by supporting Mama. "Listen, Carole, your mother can't take any more battles with you. She cries all night at the thought of your living in California. Don't put up a fuss now."

"But, Daddy, this is supposed to be the most important day of my life. I dreamed of a beautiful wedding with all our family and friends there, dancing under the colorful revolving globe." As I talked, I could feel the tears struggling to come out along with the compulsion to crawl into my father's lap to be comforted, but I knew it was no longer possible to play Daddy's little girl.

Daddy smiled wanly, "It's really our big day, too, sweetheart. Not only are you leaving to get married, you will be living far away from us. Who else will ask me to talk about history any more?"

His smile, meant to tease me into smiling back, only filled me with guilt. Then I thought again of Uncle Sherman's crude way of squeezing his sisters-in law and of patting me on my bottom. "Uncle Bernard can't be expected to discuss anything with Aunt Hester and Uncle Sherman. They don't have any interest in the arts. Uncle Sherman will just have another drink and invite Uncle Bernard to come to his shop and see how he makes all his money." I was wound up now, seeing Aunt Hester in a bright red dress with feathers around her neck and great big fake rings on her fingers with their red nails. "Can you imagine Aunt Hester advising Aunt Ruby on how to arrange her hair and put on makeup? My whole wedding will be spoiled."

Daddy sat back in his armchair and looked at me as if I were a stranger. When he spoke, his words hurt. "And since when do you sit in judgment of your family? Is that what we sent you to the university for? You who plan to teach children, are you a snob who looks down on her own family?"

I tried to fight back, "So many times I heard you call Uncle Sherman a boor, and Aunt Hester Mama's rudest sister. You laughed at them because they made their money in the needle trade. So who's the snob, Daddy? You brought us up to respect your brother, and you pointed to his children and told Michael and me to make you proud the way they make Uncle Bernard proud."

Daddy nodded slowly and said, "It may be that I said all those things to you, but I thought you knew that I never had contempt for anyone in Mama's family. They love each other, but more to the point, they love you. Would you insult them by seating them with strangers?"

I stood up and paced the room, trying to discover ways to turn around Daddy's harsh reaction to my pleas. I wanted him to be on my side, the way he so often was. "I hardly know Aunt Hester. Of all my aunts and uncles, she is the one who is most like a stranger to me. Why should she spoil my wedding?"

I heard Mama come in and turned to see her eyes glisten with unshed tears. "She may be a stranger to you, my daughter, but she has always been a good sister to me. She took care of me when I had the flu during the terrible epidemic. Every day she came and sat at my bedside, begging me to eat a little and changing the compresses on my forehead.

"You never told me that before," I protested.

Mama rode over me as if I were a mere pebble in her path. "I don't tell you everything. My sister and her husband helped us after your father lost all three of his pharmacies. But Uncle Bernard, as much as we love him, refused to give Daddy a loan, telling him he shouldn't have bought the extra stores."

I heard my father groan and his face clouded over, but he nodded and said, "Your mother is telling you the truth. Of course I admire my brother's education, but it was your mother's family that allowed us to live with them, and it was Uncle Sherman who brought over a check every week so we could pay the rent and buy food for the family."

They had both defeated me with their family memories. Yet I held on to my stubborn belief that they were sentimental and unrealistic. Uncle Bernard deserved more loyalty from my parents. Did they forget the long trips he made to take care of us when we were sick? I would watch his table at the reception and make sure Uncle Sherman didn't make a total fool of himself. How he loved to slap his male friends on the back and laugh at all his own jokes. My parents just didn't understand.

After the ceremony, Jack and I were swept away in a cheering crowd of our own friends and young cousins.

The small dance floor creaked under the stomping feet of so many dancers. September heat sent beads of sweat down my face, frizzing my newly permed hair and leaving damp circles on the satin dress that was so perfect a few hours before.

Mama and Daddy chatted happily with their friends and relatives. Mama looked so young in her blue lace gown, but Daddy looked simply uncomfortable in the tuxedo he had hated to rent. Jack and I danced until my feet would no longer take orders from my brain.

While I rested, I glanced over to Uncle Bernard's table and my mouth dropped open. There he sat, his arm around Aunt Hester who, by some miracle, did not smoke and who looked exotic in a slim gray gown that matched the gray of her hair. When the revolving globe sent its light out, Aunt Hester appeared particularly beautiful as pink and blue sparkles danced around her head. There was Uncle Sherman bowing low over Aunt Ruby's hand after dancing two dances with her. This was an Uncle Sherman I didn't recognize.

All the tension of the past weeks disappeared. Before the night was over, it no longer surprised me to see Uncle Bernard and Uncle Sherman lead the rest of the men in a slow, graceful dance, their heads held high with pride, their hands holding the white handkerchief that joined them as they bent low and then raised their bodies up in perfect unison. Their legs reached first in front, then in back, their eyes closed in some shared memory of this loving tribute to bride, groom, and to the traditions that were older than any of us could remember.

Who could have known this would happen? Mama's strong arms surrounded me. "I love you, sweet daughter. May God watch over you and give you a beautiful life."

I would miss her terribly.

An April Ceremony

"You have a beautiful baby boy," the nurse exclaimed, handing me the tiny bundle of red-faced fury. Later, everyone in the family applauded. A boy! Mama glowed with happiness when Jack handed her our first born the day we came home from the hospital. I sighed with relief knowing that Mama would be with me during the early weeks of parenthood.

Of course, Mama wasn't the only helper in that first week. Jack insisted on taking time off. "After all," he said, "I want to be near my son the first seven days of his life. I won't be in your way. I'll shop and do the chores no one else has the time to do."

My heart started to ache--seven days held a special meaning, for on the eighth day our sweet little baby would be the guest of honor at his bris. Mama's arms tightened around the baby, and I realized that she, too, was thinking of the circumcision, the ritual for a Jewish infant boy that followed the ancient tradition.

"You must hire a nurse to take care of our baby," Mama commanded.

Jack gave me a look that said, "You handle this problem."

The problem consisted of the fact that we were already three adults and one tiny baby in a one bedroom, one bath apartment filled with all the paraphernalia that the baby needed.

"Mama," I ventured, "I think that you and I could learn to take care of the baby. The hospital gave us a booklet with all the instructions for the baby's comfort after the circumcision."

Mama's lips curled in disdain. "A booklet can't tell you when a tiny baby is in pain. My grandson deserves to have professional help. Your father and I will pay for the nurse's services."

It hadn't been easy for Mama to leave home and come to California for the birth of her first grandchild. Because she felt guilty about leaving Daddy and my brother, letters went back and forth until she finally made up her mind. Her last letter made Jack sit back in shock. "Read that sentence again, " he said, holding his head.

I swallowed and read, "Yes, my darling daughter, I will come to help you with this wonderful blessing, but I can't stay more than six weeks."

"Six weeks." Jack rolled his eyes toward the ceiling and whistled softly. "Can you imagine your mother sleeping in the living room for six weeks? The day bed is not the most comfortable in the world."

So miserable were the last weeks of pregnancy that I could barely take a deep breath. But I tried to make soothing sounds for Jack's sake. "She'll be such a help. I won't have time to fuss over meals or do the ironing. Mama will take over."

"Yes," Jack agreed, resignation underlining every word. "She certainly will."

And she did, but I refused to complain. Mama cooked, cleaned, and fussed over me until I practically purred with pleasure. We interviewed several nurses friends had recommended for the position. "She'll only have to stay a few days after the bris," I assured Jack.

Mama and I voted for Mrs. Bellamy because she fell in love with the baby the minute she set eyes on him. Jack made funny faces when we heard Mrs. Bellamy cooing over the baby and saying, "Him is so bootiful!" Mama saw nothing wrong with anything that Mrs. Bellamy did, as long as those experienced hands were changing diapers, feeding a screaming baby, and soothing him to sleep.

I apologized to Mrs. Bellamy about the rented rollaway bed, and the fact that she and Mama would both have to sleep in the living room. "Don't worry your young head," she said, pushing the rollaway as close to our bedroom door as possible. "This way I'll hear the baby when he cries."

Diapers and bottles took over the small apartment. We had a nursery, but little space to sit down.

Jack made the necessary phone calls for the bris, including speaking to the rabbi and the mohel, whose specialty was to perform the delicate surgery. I trusted the mohel and I trusted Mama. After all, she had gone through the ceremony years ago when my brother was born.

But Jack and I had misgivings the night before the bris. We lied to each other. "It can't hurt. Millions of babies have survived the shock. Besides, he'll like the drop of wine the mohel gives him."

"You're right, darling. Do you remember your own bris?"

Jack grimaced, but said, "Of course not. It's been years, silly."

Even so, his face was a confused blend of pride and concern as he clutched the baby closer to him. I watched him placing the baby back in his crib and wondered if he were remembering his mother who had died a year before. Jack stood there quietly as if he were worshipping at the shrine of something even he could not quite comprehend. "He's a little miracle," Jack said with tears in his eyes. I held my breath, caught up in the poetry of the moment. Surely no one else in the universe had loved a baby the way my husband and I loved our son.

In the morning, I had trouble controlling my mixed emotions. I turned to Mama and cried. "How can we allow our baby to be hurt just to follow some old tradition?"

Mama passed her hand over my head, as if she were blessing me. "Darling, our baby is in a long line of babies that have followed this tradition since the time of Abraham. Do you want to break that line?"

I shook my head, but the tears wouldn't stop, and
Mama, too, had to wipe her eyes on her apron. All three of
us held on to our misery, and no one could look at Mrs.
Bellamy, who sighed loudly every few minutes.

The ceremony was set for eleven o'clock in the
morning, and Mama moved quietly around, pushing a
square wooden table into the terribly crowded room. The
only sounds were of the baby's vigorous sucking and Mrs.
Bellamy's whispered endearments.

I had called our friends to invite them to the
ceremony and to share refreshments afterwards. Jack, pale
and silent, brought in sliced meats, cake, and cookies,
which Mama arranged on the white, embroidered tablecloth
she had purchased in New York. She held her face taut
and emotionless, as if some force outside of her controlled
her movements and feelings.

Mrs. Bellamy, red-eyed and tired, informed us that
she would leave the house while the "cutting" was going
on, but that she would be back as soon as the baby needed
her. Before she left, she lingered over the baby, tenderly
diapering him and dropping kisses on his bare legs.

I longed for Jack's touch, but he avoided me.
Instead, he followed Mama's instructions to take down the
goblets and the wine, which she set up on the table, along
with the food and plates we would need to serve our
guests. Jack placed the traditional yarmulke on his head
and wrapped himself in the silky prayer shawl he had worn
at his Bar Mitzvah. I envied his ceremonial dress and
wished for the long and voluminous robes I had seen
women wear in pictures of biblical times.

I wanted to wrap my still aching body in material
that would cover the wound I felt everyone could see. It
had taken so many hours to coax my baby into the world;
would he ever forgive me for the pain he would suffer? I
kissed the nape of his neck, and lifted up his tiny hand to
admire its perfection for the hundredth time as he curled it

once more beneath his chin. From some stony place around my heart came the promise, " I will never again allow anything to hurt you." It was to be my pledge.

The sound of the doorbell broke the spell of silence, as friends pushed their way into the room, laughing at the tiny space left for them to stand. Everyone took turns congratulating Jack and me after peeking at the baby sleeping in total ignorance of his importance on this April morning.

The rabbi and the mohel entered the room with bustling good cheer. Wedged between the guests and the clean table holding the baby's bassinet, they signaled that they were prepared to start the blessings. Mama shepherded the women into the kitchen, all but our friend Gerda who said, "Please let me stay. I have never attended a bris." Before I left, I watched Jack holding the baby in his arms while the rabbi and the mohel stood before him, chanting in Hebrew.

In the kitchen, Mama pressed a prayer book into my icy hands and caressed my back. I could hear her saying the prayers, and I kept my eyes on her, so serene in her faith. I knew that if I looked away I would give in to my desire to put my head down and weep. One friend read from her prayer book, while another wrapped her arms around her body and remained deep in thought.

Suddenly, a few sharp cries broke both the silence and the tension. I held my breath, but except for a few more whimpers, my baby was quiet. It was done, and our son took his place with all those who had endured this ritual before him.

"Drink, my daughter." Mama kissed me then held a tiny cup of wine to my dry lips. "Your son will be fine. He was brave and only cried a moment before he, too, sipped the good, sweet wine."

Gerda, who witnessed the ceremony, came in with uneven steps before she sat down hard on a kitchen chair.

"It was wonderful, but I feel weak... my husband almost fainted." The women joined the men, laughing, drinking, eating--relieved that the ceremony was over.

Mrs. Bellamy couldn't have gone far, for she popped into the room, took the baby in her arms and, cradled him tenderly, went into the bedroom--but not before she shot a baleful look at the unsuspecting mohel. I smiled, hearing her crooning over the baby, "Him is such a good boy!" Bless you, Mrs. Bellamy, "him" is, I thought.

Jack searched for me and swept me into his arms. We felt that we had passed a crisis in our lives. Unconcerned with the laughter around us, we embraced. I stroked my husband's face and said, "I promise you, sweetheart, our baby will be the last son who will suffer pain because of some ancient tradition. We have done our duty. Next time, no parties, no crowds-- just the necessary procedure in the hospital soon after birth." Jack hugged and kissed me again.

And that's the way it was when we brought two more sons into the world. Mrs. Bellamy and I were in complete agreement. I suspect even Mama agreed.

1954   Dr. Greenberg--Help Me!

"Can you help me, Dr. Greenberg?" Even as I spoke, I pulled the skimpy cotton gown around me, conscious of my half-nude body, quickly sat up on the examining table and looked at our family doctor. He was a heavy-set man who seemed older than his forty-some years. Mama said that he tried to help everyone and would die young because of it. "Mark my words. The man looks like he hasn't had a good night's sleep in ages."

I remembered her words and felt guilty taking up his time when I was no longer a patient of his. But my emotions were so chaotic that I had to have an answer to my problem right away. Dr. Greenberg put an arm around me and said, "Maybe you're not really pregnant, only late." I leaned against his substantial body and shook my head.

"No. I'm never late. When I had my first baby, I was sure I was pregnant, and I'm sure this time, too."

"How old is your baby?"

I started to cry. "Only a few months past his first birthday. He's such a demanding child. I just can't have another baby so soon."

Dr. Greenberg let me cry. I needed to express my pent-up anxiety and fear since last week when I had missed my second period. Jack and I were visiting Mama and Daddy with the hope of moving back to New York if Jack could find a better job. We missed our families so much, and this might be the last opportunity we had to make the move.

"God, honey," Jack said, "This isn't the time to have another baby."

"I didn't conceive him all by myself." Anger flashed between us until Jack reached out for me and held me in his arms as if I were the baby I carried inside of me.

When I confided our plight to my brother, Michael offered to drive me to see Dr. Greenberg. In the doctor's office, I let my tears dry and my legs touch the floor as I climbed down from the worn, plastic-topped examining table. A few folding chairs and a small white table completed the furnishings in the room. Dr. Greenberg's office was part of his regular apartment, and I felt conspicuous walking past the mothers and children sitting outside the building. Luckily we were outside of Mama's neighborhood. The women there would have no problem asking me personal questions.

Even in this neighborhood, I felt the women were staring at me with disapproving eyes. I imagined they would grab their children close and say, "Shame on her.

She doesn't want her baby." I felt safe in Dr. Greenberg's office but still ashamed of my unnatural desires. He handed me a bottle of pills and said, "Try these, Carole. They may bring on your period but don't get your hopes up."

"What if the pills don't work?" I asked, fearing his answer.

He sighed, picked up an instrument and said, "Then we'll have to go in and take the baby."

My head jerked up as if I were a puppet on a string. "Surely you can't call it a baby yet. That would mean ...." I couldn't finish my sentence. I turned my head to the wall to avoid looking at the instrument in Dr. Greenberg's hand. When he didn't answer, I turned back and tried again, "Are you telling me you'll have to perform an…an abortion? The muscles in my throat tightened, but I had said the word.

"Goodness, Carole, you aren't an innocent little girl!" The doctor's hand dropped the instrument on the shiny table where it rattled back and forth. "Of course, I would prefer that the medicine would succeed in bringing on your period, but there are no miracles here. The sooner we take care of this problem the safer for you." The lines on his forehead deepened as his impatience grew. "Now finish dressing and see me again in three days, unless...."

"Yes, I understand. I'll call you when…if my period starts."

He squeezed my shoulder. "Very well. I've got to hurry and see some really sick patients."

I caught the meaning of his words. He was right, of course. I wasn't sick, only terribly sad and confused about the thought of giving up my baby's life. For now I realized that there really was a baby inside me, not just a "problem."

I was wrapped in gloom as Michael guided the car through the heavy traffic of children coming home from school. Without thinking, my hand caressed my body where moments of passion had created life. Michael understood my silence.

"Will you tell Mama about seeing Dr. Goldberg?" Michael asked.

"Probably. That way I don't have to lie about my morning queasiness. She's been so good about taking care of the baby and letting me sleep every morning."

"Okay, but you don't have to bring up the abortion idea yet." There he went again, always protecting Mama from the truth.

Annoyed, I snapped, "Whatever I decide to do, it will be because Jack and I have talked it over, not because Mama would be upset."

I stared out the window for the rest of the ride, not paying attention to the boys playing stickball who dashed out so close to the passing cars.

Late that night, after dinner and after fighting the usual battle to persuade the baby to go to sleep, Jack and I climbed two flights to the rooftop--the only place where we could speak privately. Warm evening air lifted the damp hair off my face and brought relief from the humid city heat. Darkness softened the harsh lines of heating ducts and the uneven brick wall at the end of the roof. I could smell the softened tar under my feet, bringing back memories of the many times Jack and I had escaped to the roof to avoid curious eyes. We needed to press our bodies close together and seek each other's lips in long shivering kisses that took away our breath.

"Don't worry, honey," Jack said. "We'll manage. Moving back here was a foolish dream. I've been out chasing down job leads all over town and nothing has materialized." He pulled me close, for he, too, remembered our heated embraces on this same spot. He kissed me, then said, "Call Dr. Greenberg in the morning and tell him we decided to have the baby."

For one brief moment, our doubts slipped away and we were able to let go of our anxiety about the future.

In the light of a morning that dawned clear and cooler, the future appeared less frightening, but telling Mama about my pregnancy presented another challenge. Jack called the doctor for me while I asked Mama to sit in the living room to talk.

She dropped heavily into her favorite chair. For the first time during this hectic visit, I noticed that Mama looked older, her back not as straight, her hair showing more gray than I remembered from our last visit. Even the lines on both sides of her thin nose had become more pronounced, emphasizing her tired and concerned expression. Guilt caused me to notice that everything about the living room looked worn, too; the flowers on the slipcovers had faded into indistinct shapes, and Daddy's big, overstuffed chair listed a bit to one side. Mama's practical, dry voice brought me back to my present task: "Well, what is so important, my daughter, that I have to stop my day's work and sit in the living room so early in the morning?"

I smiled at Mama's belief that the kitchen was for family while the living room was for guests and special occasions. No wonder so many of my memories and even my dreams returned to the kitchen. I avoided directly answering her question by only saying, "It's cooler in here, and maybe you'll stop thinking of all the things you have to do."

She twitched a bit in annoyance. "Even if I don't think about them, they will still be there for me to do."

Properly chastised for my comment, I hastened to the subject pressing on my mind. "I have news for you, Mama, and I know we will need to spend a few more minutes together." I hesitated, felt a wave of nausea that threatened my resolve, but continued, "I am going to have another baby, so Jack and I have decided not to move back here."

Mama absorbed the news in disturbing silence. Two red spots that suddenly appeared in the whiteness of her cheeks alerted me to the depths of her emotions. Her eyes behind her glasses shut me out. I hurried on, hoping to create a soothing sound in the emptiness that surrounded Mama. "It will be hard at first with two little ones, but Jack is so good about helping me. We'll have to find a larger apartment, of course, maybe even a small house, but ...." I heard my hopeful voice and the enormity of my self-delusion hit me. A larger place? A small house? How could Jack's present salary cover that plus the expenses of a new baby?

A gray shadow spread into the sun-bright room eating up the space between Mama and me. "Foolish, foolish children. You don't realize what your life will be like, two babies, no family to help…you don't understand how hard it will be." Mama said.

I groped my way across the shadow, trying to reach Mama, needing her to reassure me. But she had drifted into her memories, leaving me alone and frightened. Her voice came through in tight little spasms. "It was horrible. You were my baby, but I felt as if you belonged to someone else." I held my breath, wanting to hear every word, but dreading it as well. "You cried all day and all night. I didn't have enough milk so I cried, too. I looked at you and wished that I had never given birth. Too much to expect from one person. My beautiful little son. I wanted to hold him and feed him. My sisters came and took care of me. Sometimes I didn't know who I was."

I stared at Mama, locked with her into the past. "Mama, don't talk like this. You frighten me."

She didn't even turn her head to look at me, only clutched herself around the middle.

Once again she spoke. "I didn't want another baby. I prayed that God would take away my pain."

Tears fell from my eyes, but I ignored them. Mama had to see me. She sat quietly, then sighed. She lifted her arms, and for a second I wanted to flinch, but she whispered, "May the Lord bless you and give you strength."

I knew then that I would love this baby even more. Mama had blessed us both.

1957   Demons in Mama's Purse

I was never totally free of family concerns, even in faraway California. One night, while Jack slept, I awoke sweating and trembling. For in my dream I had opened Mama's little worn brown purse and out of it swarmed alligators, dinosaurs, snakes, and lizards. What was the dream trying to tell me? Perhaps it was trying to challenge me to rid myself of the demons of my past, the ones that had to do with Mama.

The demons were busy that night when I left my home in California to join the family in the Bronx to discuss "the problem of Uncle Harry's will," as Uncle Sam put it in his phone call. His dining room was more like a war room. That's the way it looked - the opposing forces lined up on either side of a big walnut dining table. There was Mama, sitting white and pinch-faced with me and my brother behind her. (Daddy had said, "Leave me out of your family's mess!") Across the table sat Uncle Sam and Aunt Alice Sam's--we called her this to make it clear she was not Mama's sister Alice. Next to Uncle Sam on the other side sat my two cousins, a quietly determined Judy and Sarah, who, like myself, had flown in from California. They were the reason the family came together. Judy tried to look confident, but there were two bright spots on her cheeks, and Sarah's nervous fingers constantly smoothed down her curly brown hair. Mama kept opening and closing the gold clasp on her little purse.

"Marsha," Aunt Goldie said, for she and my other aunts had just come in from the kitchen, "please stop snapping that purse." Mama put down her purse but kept one hand on it while giving her sister a sour look. I found myself staring at the purse, glancing away, but being drawn to it once more. Years ago, when I was a curious little girl, Mama warned me never to touch her purse. Even now, as a grown woman with three children, the purse fascinated me.

The three younger sisters carefully chose seats away from the warring parties. "Okay," said Uncle Sam, his round, kind face pulled into a grim mask, "we must settle Harry's estate here—not in court."

Mama's voice came out dry and controlled, unlike the hysteria I had witnessed several months ago when news of Uncle Harry's death brought me home to help Mama. "Harry, little brother Harry, after all your suffering, you're gone." She had rocked back and forth; tears poured down her face.

"There is no problem. I have the answer in Harry's own handwriting." Mama said. She opened the purse and carefully took out the little sheets of paper she had saved since Uncle Harry left for California twenty years ago.

Uncle Sam made a gesture with one of his big capable hands that seemed to sweep away all of Mama's precious papers. His daughter Judy, the older of my two cousins, placed her hand over her father's and said, "We understand, Aunt Marsha, that you feel strongly about the letters Uncle Harry sent you. But Sarah and I were there in the weeks before he died. And things change."

"Exactly," Mama said, her voice cold enough to form an icy barrier between her and her nieces, who had always been close to Mama in the days when we all used to take boat rides up the Hudson River or go on picnics in the park. "Yes, you two were there when poor Harry died. What did you say to him that made him change his will?"

Aunt Alice raised her strong voice, "Marsha, you are talking about my daughters. You know my girls too well to even hint at such nastiness. They made the trip here only because they knew you were unhappy about the will, and they wanted to make everything clear." The stress in Aunt Alice's voice made her wheeze and made me feel guilty.

"Listen you two," it was little Aunt Nettie speaking to everyone's surprise. Most of the time she let Aunt Goldie be the one who spoke for her. "God forbid we should start a fight in the family. Harry didn't have that much money that we should yell and scream at each other." Next to her, Aunt Miriam nodded her head and yawned. None of this seemed terribly important to her.

Mama turned her head slowly. I could almost hear machinery creak--so unreal did she look and act. "Nettie, the amount of money is not the question; what is right or wrong is. You know that Harry wrote over and over that I was the one to take charge of his money after he ...." Mama's voice trembled precariously and I suddenly saw her again as the little girl leaving Horadisht with her brother. So many years had passed, but Mama told me that she never forgot her promise to watch over Harry. Poor man, so sick all these years. Mama cried every time she remembered how her brother was turned away at Ellis Island because of his health. "He looked so lost after they separated him from me when we left the ship. Bubbie *begged* them to let him stay with her, but she couldn't make herself understood." Yet it was hard to think of Mama as a little girl when I noticed the harsh facial expression she had when she looked at Judy and Sarah.

Mama straightened her back in the chair and composed herself. Sarah tried once more to reason with her. "We don't want to start a family argument. Uncle

Harry asked us to take down his last wishes. We had two people from the hospital as witnesses."

Oddly enough, Mama made the same gesture with her hand that Uncle Sam had made a short time before. "Don't talk to me about witnesses. Look at your Uncle's letters. Then you'll know why I can't accept your..." she hesitated, then finished strongly, "lies."

Uncle Sam slammed his fist down on the table and made Mama's little purse bounce. "You will not call my daughters liars in my house!"

Judy broke in, "Aunt Marsha, we are only trying to do what Uncle Harry's lawyer told us to do. Please try to understand. We need the bonds Uncle Harry left in your keeping before we can settle the estate." Sarah nodded, but her face revealed her tension and anger. I trusted both of my cousins and leaned forward to speak to Mama.

She turned to me, her eyes dark and questioning. "What do you think of your cousins, my daughter? Isn't this a shame? My Papa would not accept such family *tsouris.*"

I knew enough Yiddish to realize she meant trouble, but once again I wondered why she always slipped back to those childhood days with my grandfather. I choked back the argument I was about to give her--that a last will witnessed and signed *had* to be acknowledged as a legal one. Instead I shook my head and responded, "Sleep on it, Mama. Speak to the family when you are more calm."

"I am perfectly calm, my daughter. Have you ever known your mother to be against the family?"

I had no answer. Of course she wasn't against the family. To everyone she symbolized the family, especially since Bubbie had died a few years before. And I, her only daughter, did not have the guts to tell her that she was wrong! My brother shook his head and shrugged. He had given up the battle a long time ago.

Aunt Goldie, often the peacemaker in family disagreements, spoke to Mama in a conciliatory tone, "How about making two lists showing how much Harry wanted to leave to each one, one list from your letters and the other from the will that Judy has. Then maybe the differences won't seem so terrible."

Mama rose from her chair. "Obviously, you don't trust me. A will from a dying man, surrounded by people who couldn't love him the way that I did. How many times have I read Harry's letter to you? Remember that I visited him in California, too. Nothing ever changed. Why should it change now?" She sat down again.

Aunt Goldie rolled her eyes at me. "Your crazy mother, " she often said with a laugh, "she gets an idea into her head and it won't get out. Like the way she always says that she was with Papa when he died. Nonsense!" I turned to look at Mama. Were her stories to me, so much a part of my childhood, fact or fiction? She was so sweet and gentle most of the time, but cross her and a rigid, unswerving person took her place. Which one was my real mother? Did I dare stand up for my own beliefs?

Judy interrupted my thoughts. "You must realize we have a deadline. You need to give us the bonds this week, Aunt Marsha, so we can meet that deadline." She waited for Mama's reply. When none came, she continued, "There's so little difference between the amounts you have and the new figures. Let's be sensible. Uncle Harry would want us to follow his wishes without a fight."

"No one is fighting," Mama said, her mouth thinly drawn, her fingers tense on the brown purse. "What you have is not even clear English; it's lawyers' talk. What I have are the words of my dead brother." She placed heavy emphasis on the word "dead."

I saw the pain on Uncle Sam's face. I also heard it in his voice. "After all, Harry was my brother, too. When we were kids in Horadisht, I looked out for him. I'd do his share of the work in Papa's shop many times. He wore my clothes when he came here on the boat. And when they sent him back, a part of me went with him. Don't make yourself into such a big lady--my daughters loved Harry, too. They were there at the hospital week after week when the rest of us were three thousand miles away."

"And how many times did you visit him in California? And answer me this, Sam, how come in the new will *your* daughters get money and in *my* letters they are never mentioned?" Mama spoke in a low voice.

Aunt Alice sucked in her breath; nobody else spoke. "Marsha, you should be ashamed to talk to Sam like that. Such a good brother he has been to you and your children. Could his daughters be anything but good?"

Mama stood up. There was anger in her that sent shock waves around the table. Like an old-time religious fanatic, she raised both hands in the air and whispered,"As God is my witness, I carry the truth." In one hand she held up the brown purse. I stared at it, mesmerized, pulled once again into Mama's orbit. From her stories, I knew this was the same Mama who had stretched out on her Papa's grave and willed the grass to grow up into her body. How could anyone not believe her?

Uncle Sam didn't. When Mama walked around the table, she slowly let her arms come down until she reached Uncle Sam. She put both arms around his neck. "I love you, dear brother, as we both loved Harry. Please do not push me aside. You must believe me."

Uncle Sam took her arms down from around his neck and said, "When you speak bad words against my daughters, you speak bad words against me. This cannot be the way Mama and Papa taught us to behave to each other."

Mama wept. She left their house and never spoke to her brother again. She gave the bonds to my cousins,

who were relieved to avoid a court order against Mama.
Aunt Alice and Uncle Sam moved to California shortly
after that. Mama visited me often in our northern
California home, but she didn't suggest a trip to see her
brother.

Uncle Sam died some years later. When Mama
heard the news, she went for a long walk. When she
returned, she sat quietly and read her Bible. If she grieved,
she did so in the privacy of her own heart. But the demons
remained to torment us later.

1960 Aunt Miriam--The Family Rebel

Mama was visiting me in California when we
received a letter from my cousin Dorothy telling us of Aunt
Miriam's death. It was July and we sat out on my breezy
patio while Mama set her hair with the green sticky lotion
she always used. She wiped her hands on her apron and
picked up the letter again.

"My poor sister," Mama said, crying and shaking
her head. Mama loved all her sisters, but Miriam brought
out her maternal instinct. Mama remembered her as one of
the tiny twins nestling in Bubbie's arms as the family said
goodbye to their little village. Aunt Miriam, to me,
remained young and blithe in spirit, much like her twin,
Aunt Goldie, but I sensed in her an extra edge of
independence. Could that difference be what Mama
disliked and why she thought of her sister as the black
sheep of the family?

"Aunt Miriam was fun to be with," I told Mama.

"Yes, but she didn't have a strong feeling for the
family."

Mama dabbed at her eyes and put the letter away. I
felt she was consigning her younger sister to a separate
drawer in her mind.

"I remember her big fight with her husband before the divorce," I said. "It still makes me laugh when I think of her chasing him down the hallway whacking him over the head with her purse."

Amazingly, Mama laughed out loud. "I don't remember that at all. It was just like her. But she gave up a good man and what did that get her?"

"At least she didn't waste time before she started looking for someone to replace him."

Mama turned her face to me. "I hope you don't take her actions as a proper way to live your life."

It was my turn to be surprised. "Why would I? I'm happily married. I certainly don't need to search for another man!"

Mama and I flew back to New York for the funeral. Even there, as we sat shiva in Aunt Goldie's living room, the family expressed disapproval of Aunt Miriam's rebellious ways. The mirrors were all properly covered, and we perched uncomfortably on wooden boxes. After my uncles had chanted several prayers, Aunt Goldie set out trays of cold meats, salads, and homemade cakes. She sat down and said, "What a terrible way to die. On a dance floor with a man she hardly knew."

Only Mama's sister, Aunt Alice, sighed as she munched on a cookie. "It's too bad she died young, but I wouldn't mind dying in a man's arms." Aunt Alice had just divorced her husband.

"It's better than dying an old lady forgetting how to have fun." I blurted out. My aunts clucked their tongues at me and Mama frowned.

Uncle Marvin bounced up and pulled Aunt Alice to her feet. "So come, my darling sister-in-law, let's dance and shock your sisters and my wife."

But Aunt Nettie was not shocked. "Oh, Marv," she giggled, "you're terrible. How much schnapps did you have?"

I laughed, too. "That's a great way to remember Aunt Miriam. I don't think I ever saw her cry, even when Uncle Harry died."

We were all quiet for a moment, remembering Aunt Miriam as we loved her. Aunt Goldie picked up an antique silver frame with a picture of the six sisters. She slowly wiped the glass before she set the frame down, making a place for it in front of the other family pictures on the round coffee table.

I was uncomfortable in the formal living room, so crowded with cut glass vases filled with artificial flowers and overstuffed furniture that the family hardly ever used. Somehow everything looked slightly dusty, though Aunt Goldie was a meticulous woman. I leaned over to speak to Dorothy, Aunt Miriam's daughter. "It's a pity your mother isn't here. She hated serious faces. I bet she'd come up with something to make everyone laugh."

I think I made an enemy. My cousin stood up and said, "This is ridiculous. My mother may have been different from all of you, but she doesn't deserve this kind of foolishness on the day of her funeral."

I shrugged but felt more than a little guilty when I saw Mama's disapproving eyes. Once again, I wished Aunt Miriam were with us to take away the gloom.

"None of us are saints," Aunt Goldie said, "but Miriam would make Papa roll over in his grave."

The other sisters nodded in solemn agreement. I realized they were counting the skeletons in the family closet. Uncle Marvin glanced at Aunt Nettie, then slumped down in the big armchair, as if to hide from her gaze. I had heard whispers of an affair. It was odd to be an adult and know all the family secrets, so different from my childhood innocence. I could see Mama sitting quietly on the uncomfortable box. Unlike Uncle Marvin, Mama had little to hide.

Then she abruptly took charge of the conversation. "What do you know about Papa, Goldie? You were an infant when he died. What Miriam does...." She stopped with a pained expression. "What Miriam *did* has nothing to do with family. She lived a wild life, gambling away her household money on cards and on the horses. Even so, she didn't deserve to die like that."

"Well," murmured Uncle Seymore, "that crazy business of wiping out their bank account to give money to a gypsy for a magic colorful egg was more than wild. I would have divorced her, too."

I could see Aunt Miriam, whirling around in a gauzy blue dress, made up with penciled-in eyebrows, rouge dotted high on her cheeks, and bright red lipstick on her full lips.

I had always enjoyed sitting near her during the weekly dinners at Aunt Goldie's. I'd poke her and ask her to tell me funny stories to take away my sleepy feeling after the five course family dinner.

"You could look so much prettier," she said to me when I was suffering through the awkward early teens.

"What can I do to look prettier? Mama won't let me wear any makeup. Even Daddy makes me rub off lipstick if he sees me trying to cover my mouth to hide the color. Why can't they realize I'm growing up? You let Dorothy wear lipstick."

"You can wait with the lipstick for a few years yet. But your hair," she shook her head and ran her red fingernails through my silky fine tresses. Then she smiled and looked around at her sisters, gossiping in a corner of the dining room. "Come with me into the kitchen. I don't want to listen to a lot of talk about recipes and food. I'm so full I think I'm going to burst. Sweetheart, let me show you what to do with your hair. A woman's hair can turn her into a queen."

I didn't really want to be a queen. "How about a princess? Can you give me long blond hair that grows all the way down to my knees?" She laughed and pulled me close. I enjoyed sniffing in the sweet flower scent of her perfume. From the front of her pretty red dress, I inhaled some mysterious odor that made me think of the jungle. Not like the odors of the Bronx Zoo which was near our house, but something kind of wild and musky that made me squirm in my chair without knowing why.

In the kitchen, where all the dishes sat gleaming from the scrubbing Mama had given them, we found a spot on the oilcloth-covered table for Aunt Miriam to work her magic. I ran my fingers over her eyebrows. "Why do you tweeze all your eyebrows out and then pencil in new ones?" I asked.

Aunt Miriam didn't act annoyed at my blunt question the way the other aunts might have. "Silly girl. Thin eyebrows are so popular now. You go to the movies. Look at Joan Crawford's eyebrows. She's my idol."

I knew the actress Aunt Miriam meant, but except for the eyebrows, Aunt Miriam could never be taken for Joan Crawford. I loved the movies too, but I didn't want to look like any particular star.

I watched Aunt Miriam who was busily pouring sugar and water into a fancy cut glass vase. I confided to Aunt Miriam," I heard that Aunt Nettie has a picture of Clark Gable under her pillow. Isn't that crazy? He has ears that stick out five inches at least!"

Aunt Miriam gently pushed my head over the oilcloth, protecting my clothes with a big, white dishtowel. She slowly spilled the sticky sugar water syrup over my head and laughed when I jumped as the cold liquid oozed down into my ears. While she wiped my face, she said, seriously for her, "Listen, darling, don't laugh at your aunts. Uncle Marvin is snoring out there after eating and drinking too much. At least Aunt Nettie can dream of Clark Gable, even with his big ears."

I smirked and wondered if Aunt Miriam had a picture of a man under her pillow. Since I had seen her whack my uncle over the head, my idea of married life was open to all possibilities. Mama never hit Daddy with her purse, but I could tell that her words left a mark when they came out quietly from her tight mouth.

My hair felt heavy even after Aunt Miriam combed the gooey mess through. "Aren't you going to rinse some of that stuff off? " I licked my fingers and enjoyed the sweet taste, though I felt a little guilty about wasting food on my hair.

"Stop worrying. I usually put a lotion on my own hair, but at 13 you can't afford to buy what I use. I have lots of bobby pins to set your hair. And then, you'll see, you'll look just like a movie star. And maybe you'll even have a boy's picture to put under *your* pillow." I blushed but it was a new idea for me to think about at night when I pulled fantasies out of my head to help me fall asleep.

An hour later, it was time to take out the pins and comb the springy little curls that popped up all over my head. "Do I look like Shirley Temple?" I asked hopefully.

"No, darling, just like your pretty self but with lovely curls instead of your own stick-straight hair."

I looked into the mirror Aunt Miriam held up for me. We went back to the porch where the family sat to relax. I smiled because I could see that I had everyone's attention. My hair felt pretty stiff, but I guessed that it had to be in order for the curls to last. Then I began to shake my head to see if my new curls would dance like Shirley Temple's did. I knew I was showing off, but it was fun to toss my head around just like the actresses in the movies.

"Oh my," Aunt Miriam laughed at the shower of white flakes that flew out with every shake of my head. "Look at this - it's snowing in July." She couldn't stop giggling; after a few moments of shock, I joined her, laughing until the tears ran down my face.

Mama raised her eyebrows and commented, "Really, Miriam, it's bad enough that you try to look like a Hollywood starlet, but I wish you'd think twice before you make Carole want to be something she's not. Go wash that mess out of your hair, my daughter; we can't go on the subway with you looking like that."

Aunt Miriam and I tried to hold back our laughter, but the more I giggled, the more the sugary flakes jumped off my head. Pretty soon the whole family was laughing just as hard. Even Mama.

I'd like to remember Aunt Miriam laughing and clapping her hands. It's too bad she died young, but I choose to believe that she'd prefer it to dying old, forgetting how wonderful it felt to be whirled about the dance floor by a handsome man. I know he was handsome.

I can just see her face, flushed and happy, as she leaned back into his arms, flirting and enjoying every minute.

1965   Aunt Nettie--The Little Shadow

One day, several years after Uncle Marvin's death, I was visiting with Mama, and we decided to take the train to Brooklyn to see Aunt Nettie, who still hadn't recovered from losing her much loved husband. I found it difficult to be in their apartment, for all around me were pictures of Uncle Marvin, a smiling Aunt Nettie, and my two laughing cousins. Although the apartment was pleasant enough, filled as it was with flower-covered furniture and airy white draperies, I missed my uncle's hearty laugh and the funny popping noise he made when he wanted to amuse little children.

While Mama and Aunt Nettie set out platters of cheese and bagels for lunch, I walked around the living room to look at the family pictures. My favorite was the one where Uncle Marvin lifted Aunt Nettie under her arms and held her high in the air until she begged him to let her down. The photograph caught my aunt's joy for all time. How lucky she was; she reminded me of a little girl. I remember how she laughed so hard we worried that her glasses would fall off. My cousins Miltie and Eric used to love to imitate their father. Often they would stand on either side of Aunt Nettie, each with a hand under her elbows, and then they would lift her until her feet dangled and her shoes dropped off.

Both her sons and Uncle Marvin had fussed over Aunt Nettie, treating her like some precious treasure. When she was happy, she looked like the kewpie dolls that we won at Coney Island, black hair curling around her face and pretty red lips turned up in delight. She'd giggle a young girl's giggle and say, "Oh, Marv, you're such a kidder." But her life had abruptly changed with Uncle Marvins's death.

I could see the toll that grief had taken for her formerly chubby face was thin and drawn, and her voice was even quieter than I had remembered. I helped cut the bagels and covered a tray with cream cheese and lox.

"So what's new with my cousins?" I asked. My older cousin, Milton, had recently married, and Mama had told me that Aunt Nettie chafed under the sudden loss of her son's attention.

My aunt's face took on a sour expression, and my mother shook her head at me. "Don't ask," Aunt Nettie said. "I am just furious." Her lips pursed into a child-like pout, but her eyes revealed deep anger when she said, "Would you believe what my darling son bought me for Mother's Day?"

I shook my head, knowing I was about to hear the whole story. "A carving set. Can you imagine? But I suppose his wife bought it--you know his wife, the college student." Aunt Nettie's lips curled downward in contempt, an expression that startled me for her characteristic expression was a sweet smile.

"What's so terrible about a carving set?" I asked, earning another frown from Mama.

When Aunt Nettie slumped down in her chair, the small hump on her back showed up like a bundle of pain slung across her shoulders. "A knife, a son gives his mother a knife? Sharp enough to cut into my heart." She turned to me and said, "Now that my son has a wife, he insults his mother with a knife. Wait until *your* sons grow up and marry."

Mama reached for Aunt Nettie's hand but said nothing. Sometimes the sisters knew exactly how to comfort each other. This time Mama realized she couldn't offer any words that would help Aunt Nettie. The kitchen clock ticked away the minutes as we sat in a kind of mourning. I had the strangest feeling that we were sitting shiva, not for a son, but for a mother's awareness that she was no longer the center of her child's life.

"Don't waste time worrying about my mother," Milton said when I called him. I wondered about the bitterness I heard in his voice. "You remember how my dad fussed over her because she had a minor heart ailment. Well after he died, I still paid a lot of attention to my mother, but she demanded so much from me. After all, I had a wife and we were starting a family; how could I keep running to Brooklyn to hold my mother's hand?"

When I mentioned the Mother's Day gift, he only laughed. "No matter what we gave her she would complain. I got her an aide who is like an angel to her."

"I know. I heard, but Aunt Goldie says the new

aide even pushes your mother around and sometimes hurts her."

His anger exploded over the telephone. "Goldie is getting to be a stupid old woman. Don't believe all those bubbemeinsers my mother makes up to get attention. Those sisters only love to hear bad news. They come alive when somebody gets a divorce or drops dead."

"But Milton," I protested, "they're still the same aunts who laughed and gossiped at all the family parties."

"Nah, not any more. When my father died, all the life went out of the family. When my mother tells me I neglect her, I say, 'Ma, I have a family to support. You had your life. Now I have mine.'"

"God took away my happiness," Aunt Nettie wrote to Mama, "I have nothing to live for. Milton forgets he has a sick old mother. All he cares about is business." Still, she survived.

I saw Aunt Nettie one more time. Her plump cheeks surprised me. She complained constantly about Milton, but her words had lost their bitter strength. Instead they came out in a monotonous stream. They seemed to have a life of their own, almost separate from my aunt's tired mouth.

When a stroke put her into a nursing home, it was ironic that her illness left her unable to speak. Milton told Mama and me that he visited her as often as he could. "She can't talk, Carole, but I swear to you she still remembers everything I ever did that upset her. I immediately remembered the first Mother's Day after Milton's wedding when he gave her a carving set.

When I saw him last, I showed him pictures of Mama who was bent over from osteoporosis and looked like a tiny sparrow. Milton stared at the picture for a long time. "I wanted to remember your mother serving me her wonderful chocolate cake. Why do people have to get old and ugly? All the aunts ended up looking exactly alike.

And even when they were young, all they talked about was family, family. I got sick of hearing the word."

Why was Milton so different from me? I wondered. Maybe it was because Mama was so different from Aunt Nettie. Nettie faded away, but Mama fought to live.

When Aunt Nettie died, I learned of it almost by accident when I spoke to another cousin who assumed I knew. I called Milton and said, "I feel bad that you didn't phone me; I let you know right away when my mother died."

Milton hadn't changed. "What's the big deal? They both lived to a ripe old age, gave us all a bad time and died. You and I should take care of ourselves, enjoy our grandchildren and live for today. I'm going to Florida and relax in the sun. The past is the past."

"Oh, Milton, will you ever forget those days at Coney Island when your father let all of us little kids hang on to his arms while he twirled us around?"

He was quiet. Then his voice grew soft and almost tender. "No, I won't forget. But my Pop is gone--and Mom, too. Be good to yourself, kiddo; you deserve it."

"Miltie, I'll always love you. You were like a big brother to me." I had to hang up. Milton was not the type to handle sentiment well.

No matter what my cousin said about Aunt Nettie's last years, I chose to admire the stubborn way she lived on, even after Uncle Marvin died. Yes, she had existed mainly in the shadow of her ebullient husband, but she knew more happiness in that shadow than many people know in the brightness of the sun.

A BATTLE TO THE END

1970 When Anger Erupted into Bitter Pain

Life became more complex and difficult when Mama, Daddy, and Michael moved to California seventeen years after I married and resettled in the Bay Area. At least by then I had given birth to three sons, and my husband and I found we could depend on each other rather than on our parents. Unfortunately, Mama carried her old angers about Uncle Harry's estate along with her suitcases and furniture. I carefully avoided the subject, but Mama's memory pulled us into the messy family split.

One day Mama and I sat sipping tea in her small dining room close to her even smaller kitchen. "I like this apartment because I can watch people going to work or driving by, but this kitchen is ridiculous. How I miss my big kitchen in the Bronx." Mama said.

"I know, Mama, it was like Aunt Goldie's kitchen, so big it could hold all the aunts drying dishes and gossiping. Those were such wonderful days when we would all gather to visit Bubbie."

Mama was so quiet that I looked up from my tea and asked, "What are you thinking about?"

"So many gone now, Hester, Miriam, Marvin and poor Harry," she sighed.

"And poor Uncle Sam," I replied with some misgivings. I watched Mama to catch any reaction. Her lips thinned out against her teeth. That was a warning to me about pursuing the subject any further. We hadn't talked about Uncle Sam's death, even though I thought about him and my cousins, who lived only an hour from Northern California by plane. I hurried to add, "But we have so many memories of the good old days."

"Yes, they were good days until your cousins broke my heart."

"Oh, really, Mama, " I said, annoyed at this uncomfortable return to worked-over territory, "that's all finished."

"Never, my daughter, not while I have breath in my body."

I frowned. Had she always spoken so melodramatically while I was growing up? "By now Judy and Sarah probably don't even remember the whole fuss, and we've all named our last babies after Uncle Harry." I hoped mention of the children would deflect Mama's irritation and soften the harsh lines around her mouth.

"You sound as if you agree with your cousins." Mama caught me unprepared for a frontal attack. I felt a nervous tremor move through my chest.

"Let's talk about something more pleasant." Could she hear the strain in my voice?

"I never questioned my children's loyalty. Was I wrong?" She sat up straighter, her back rigid against the chair. It was so quiet in the room. I could hear the late afternoon traffic streaming past Mama's apartment house. Then her voice came from some dark place inside her, "Do you side with your cousins?"

In that moment, I was a little girl again, staring at Mama, whose eyes pinned me down like a fragile butterfly struggling to be free. A bitter taste filled my throat. Mama's face was accusing and stiff. Am I in front of God on the final Judgment Day? It was impossible to hold back my pent-up anger.

`"Yes, you were wrong. Foolishly wrong. Your nieces never did anything dishonest, yet you accused them of lying and even stealing."

Her white lips trembled, and her hands made a threatening gesture toward me. I instinctively backed away. Would she dare to hit me? If she did--I couldn't finish the thought.

"They were cheats! And all these years you've lied to me."

"I've never lied, Mama. I just avoided taking sides. I wouldn't have said anything even now, but I'm so sick of this foolish family feud." I hesitated, but the words, denied for so long, could no longer be withheld. "Because of hatred, you turned your back on Uncle Sam. Because of hatred, you have forgotten your Papa's words." I needed to tell her that for, suddenly, I realized that in betraying him, she had also betrayed the romantic child who couldn't bear to let the beautiful old story go.

" 'Family, family,' he told you. 'Family is everything.' Remember?"

Mama's face crumpled into soft, aging lines. Two tears found their way from behind the wall of her glasses and moved slowly down to the corners of her mouth. When I reached over to wipe them away, she struck my hand down and stood up. Mama, though bent over and old, managed to look forbidding yet dignified, as she left me for the sanctuary of her bedroom. As always, I struggled with guilt, but for the first time I had stood up to Mama and dared to be myself. But the biggest test was yet to come.

It didn't come right away. The phone would always ring in the late afternoon when I was so tired from a long day teaching school. I wanted nothing more than to stay home and rest in bed, when her voice, weak and frightened, would whisper, "I feel sick, my daughter." Always the dutiful daughter, I popped a tranquilizer and ran to her, praying that she would marshal her strength and survive my worst fears.

Mama and I had to face one more terrible test that ripped apart my years of loyalty and love. My own sense of safety shattered into fragments one night when I awakened to hear a pounding at the door. Who? What? I roused my husband from sleep, pulled a robe around me and opened the front door. There facing me in silence was my next door neighbor, a raincoat over her nightclothes and two serious young police officers. The rain, which had started before we went to sleep, now slashed over the plants and the little rug exposed to its fury. I invited the three indoors, wondering if my neighbor was in some terrible trouble, so anguished was her expression.

Still in a hazy half-sleep, I stood waiting for some explanation for this strange visit. I could feel my husband's body pressing close to mine. One of the policemen spoke, "I'm sorry, Ma'am, your son was killed in a car accident a few hours ago." He stammered as he spoke, and I found myself feeling oddly sorry for him.

I was dimly aware of my husband's sharp intake of breath as he turned abruptly and returned to our bedroom. But I stood in my shadowy entry hall and, like some character in a melodrama, I turned to face the wall and cried out, "Oh, no! No, dear God! There must be a mistake!" I was drowning in sorrow, chaotic pieces of thoughts racing through my brain, but I pulled myself together enough to whisper in a shaking voice that sounded strange to my ears, "How?" That's all I could manage.

"He and the other kids in the van were sleeping." The policeman spoke with some authority now that he could simply recite the facts: a torrential storm, a tired driver too anxious to get away from the dreary desert vacation spot in this awful weather, the kids, all students at a local college, never knew the horror of the huge truck that appeared out of the dark, rainy night and smashed into the van.

Somehow I survived the night, held my stone-cold husband in my arms, terrified that he would join my son in death. My youngest son shivered in shock and asked to sleep with Jack and me. There was no sleep for any of us, however. Our middle son, who had suddenly become the older son, responded to the news with a dry-eyed comment, "These things happen, Mom." He never cried, only turned his face to the wall. Outside the rain continued relentlessly to drench the soil, matching the intensity of our sorrow.

Morning came. Friends crowded our home to share our grief. Mama must be told, but I swallowed another pill and asked a close friend and the Rabbi to go to her. When she arrived at my door, held up by my white-faced brother, she broke down and came close to falling. Weeping, I said, "Come to my bedroom, Mama. You can be with me. You can see the others later." I all but carried her down the hallway as she walked on unsteady feet.

We sat together on my bed, but I reeled back when I saw the fierceness of her expression. What had I done? Her voice, crackling and almost impossible to hear, lashed out at me as if she were some avenging angel and I were her victim. "You should never have let him go on that trip. My beautiful grandson is gone forever."

We were mourners together. I had lost my son. Why didn't she take me in her arms as she had when I was a little girl weeping over some real or imagined problem? I wept again, wringing my hands, then stretching them out toward her, "Don't say that, Mama. Please. Children have to leave home. He was 18 years old...." I couldn't finish for her eyes reflected what we both saw: a tall, bony young man, so eager to leave, so shy in his attempts to say goodbye. I had reached up to touch his cheek and to tease him about the stubble on his face. I stroked his arms and kissed him, suddenly shy myself with this son who loved me with his eyes but could never find the words to express his feelings.

I heard Mama's voice, but I wanted to remain with my last thoughts of my boy, as if by remembering him alive, he couldn't possibly die. Then I could no longer protect myself from Mama's words.

"So good. So smart. He told me things he never told you. When I visited before we moved here, I'd find him outside my bedroom door waiting for me to wake up." Mama revealed.

I knew this first grandchild was very precious to her, but the child in me wondered if she remembered all the times during my childhood that I, too, had slept on the floor beside her bed, hoping that she would find me and welcome me into her arms. Did she treasure *those* memories?

When I looked at her, I found her staring at me, her eyes dark caverns of brooding misery. "Mama, we all loved him. We need to help each other." What I was really saying was "Mama, hold me, I hurt."

"My daughter, what do you know of loss and love? I loved him more than you did."

"What--what did you say?" I grabbed her arm, only to have her pull herself free. Her words reverberated in my head. I stood up and slowly moved away from her. "Don't you *ever* say that to me again!"

I breathed in short gasps, each word falling from my mouth, like ice cubes from a deep freeze. I moved to the door, looked back at her, sitting like a bundle of abandoned clothes, and spoke through stiff lips, "I will send the Rabbi to speak to you. I must be with the rest of my family and friends."

Mama and I recovered slowly from that crucial break in our relationship. I wanted nothing from her any more; not even the love that she parceled out to the deserving few. For a while, anger replaced the sharp agony I endured every time I thought of our son. There would be a time to love again, but not yet.

1972   Aunt Alice-Trouble for Daddy

Mama and Daddy had been in California for a few years when a crisis erupted just before their fiftieth anniversary. Daddy's old jealousy about Mama's close relationship with Aunt Alice flared up into a ridiculous argument that destroyed family peace.

Aunt Alice demanded so much from Mama, and Mama rarely refused her requests. Daddy and I totally agreed that Mama's love for her older sister made our little family suffer. His frustrating irritation with Aunt Alice became hatred that over the years separated him from Mama, almost to the very end.

When I was still living at home in the Bronx, I didn't hate Aunt Alice but I felt sorry for Daddy. All too often, the message was the same.

"Carole, Aunt Alice called. She's very sick and needs me to be there until she has an operation and comes out of the hospital." Mama's face was white with anxiety, for in our family illness was treated like an enemy, one to be feared and respected. I was twenty and served as Mama's backup if she was called to leave for any length of time.

Daddy was sitting at the kitchen table, eating dinner. I could feel the tension in the room. "Don't worry, Mama, I will do the cooking until you come home. I only hope that Daddy can survive if I have to be the cook." Still no sound from Daddy. I was trying to be funny, but my laugh stuck in my throat.

"I realize helping out will not be easy for you, dear. I wouldn't ask you to give up your time if it weren't a family emergency. Aunt Alice only calls me when she's very sick." Mama was speaking to me, but her eyes were on Daddy. I could hear him chewing and swallowing, but he did not respond to anything Mama said.

I wanted to help them both, so I moved close enough to Daddy to put my hand on his shoulder and said,

"Daddy, you and I will struggle to do without Mama for a while." For the first time, he stopped eating and sat clenching and unclenching his fist. After a silence that simply roared around the room, he spoke. "Marsha, if you go running to Alice one more time, I may not be here when you come home."

"Jacob, I never thought of you as cruel before, but what you said is not worthy of you." Mama stood rooted to one spot, her cheeks red in the strange whiteness of the rest of her face. Did they even remember that I was in the kitchen with them?

My stomach knotted and my breath came with difficulty. I had to reach behind me for the closest chair to fall into. Please, dear God, don't let this happen again, I prayed. I suspected Mama's thoughts were similar to mine, but her stubborn need to help her sister must have given her the strength to face my father's wrath.

"I will not tolerate your leaving our family every time that woman picks up the phone." Daddy's voice shook with a strangled sort of passion. He was trying to contain the fury that fought to explode and destroy all three of us. He sucked in his breath and said loudly, "For God's sake, Marsha. I didn't marry your sister. Her husband can afford to pay for help in the house. Carole has other responsibilities. I do not want her doing what is *your* duty. That's all I am going to say."

The spots in Mama's cheeks took on a life of their own. In my nervous fear, I couldn't stop staring at Mama's face. She twisted her apron into a tight wad between her fingers, draining all the blood from them. When she spoke, I could barely hear her words, but they had the sound of iron being struck on the pavement. "No one has the right to tell me what my responsibilities are. This family has been my life, but when there is trouble with my sisters or my brothers, it is God's law that I must respond to. I am going, Jacob."

My father stood up slowly, looked at my mother, banged his fists down on the table, then reached deliberately under the table so that it lifted up while he stared at Mama. It came smashing down when he let go. My hands flew up to cover my ears. I knew what was coming. A mad scream issued from Daddy's mouth, the words all but lost in the tumult that surrounded them. "I will not stand for a woman who will not listen to reason!" His face was more purple than red, and his eyes bulged, two brown stones ready to fling at his enemy.

"Jacob, lower your voice, please. Shouting like a crazy person will not change anything, but it could put you in the hospital or worse." Mama kept her distance, but she had the ability to use her voice the way a cowboy used a lariat, and at this moment she used that power on Daddy.

Daddy fell back into his seat as if someone had pushed him down like a deflated doll. He terrified me more in his stillness than he had in the violent screaming. He stared at Mama as if she were a stranger. Then in a whisper that struggled to come out from frozen lips, he said, "I will not speak to you again."

When he had left the room, Mama breathed again and put her arms around me. Suddenly I was her little girl again, needing her touch to take away fear. "Don't worry, Carole. He will come around. We have seen his rages before, haven't we darling? And he always returns to the loving, decent man we depend on."

"Mama, Mama, I was so afraid. All I could think of was that he could die of a stroke. What would we do?" I could not stem the tears that fell unchecked and unnoticed. "Will he divorce you? I have never seen him this angry."

"He will do no such thing. And I know what it's like to lose a father. You have heard my stories of my Papa, and it is my Papa's words that make me go to your aunt. She is family and family is sacred."

I did not want to hear Mama's old story from her childhood. I could not deny that my strongest emotion at this moment was anger at Mama. How dare she put Aunt Alice before Daddy? I pulled myself out of her arms and went to look for my father. He was sitting in his favorite club chair, holding his fingers over his pulse.

I sat down on the hassock in front of him and kissed his hand. "You are more important to me than any man in the world. I love you, Daddy, and need you to be well and part of my life." My tears flowed again, but this time they were healing for the two of us. Once again, I found myself hating Mama for her stubborn need to put her family before everything.

"Thank you, sweetheart. I am lucky I have you to talk to, but I am really sorry you had to see me lose control. There are times when a man has to take a stand. Your mother and I love one another, but her loyalty to your Aunt Alice tears me to pieces. She must make her choice."

Mama made her choice. She went to take care of Aunt Alice, and her marriage suffered for all the years that followed. The anger remained long after the occasion that provoked it. One month before Mama and Daddy were to celebrate their fiftieth wedding anniversary, I visited them in their California apartment. "Mama, your party is so close. We need to make a list of the people you want to come. Do you think some of the family will fly out here?"

My father sat at the round kitchen table, reading his paper and drinking his coffee, a favorite way to pass his afternoons. He grunted and said with characteristic sarcasm, "That bunch? Don't hold your breath! New York City is the only place on the map to them. Goldie and Nettie can afford to fly out here, but Nettie shivers when you mention flying. You can bet that Goldie won't come without her. Some sisters you have."

Mama sniffed disdainfully from her seat across from Daddy. She folded her hands in front of her and asked, "So who would come from your side of the family?" When Daddy didn't answer, she turned to me and said, "Suddenly, he loses his voice."

Sadness dragged at my heart. What had happened to the two of them that turned almost every exchange into a challenge at best and a battle at the worst? "Listen, you two, no more arguing. We need to start our lists and then decide where to have the party. Fifty years of marriage has to be special for everyone." I put false enthusiasm into my voice, hoping to change the atmosphere.

Daddy looked up at Mama, and I felt a definite sense that trouble hovered around us. I shook my head at Daddy who grinned in a humorless way and opened the wound. "And your precious sister Alice, will she come to be with her dearest sister in all the world?" Mama stood up and began to take the dishes into her tiny kitchen, so different from our big, white kitchen in the Bronx. She ignored my father and walked with a limp from the spinal arthritis that made her old age so full of pain.

"Who knows, Daddy, maybe Aunt Alice will come with her new husband."

"Now which husband is that? The third or the fourth? The first one was smart enough to leave her for another woman."

"Dad," I warned, "We don't want to bring up all that old stuff, especially now." Could he hear the pleading in my voice? There were times that I came home totally wiped out from being the buffer in their war zone.

My mother stood at the sink with her back to us, washing the cups and ignoring my father's sarcasm. "Alice will be here if she is well enough."

My father jumped into the opening, "Maybe she'll send you a telegram and ask you to come help her if she has a headache or an ingrown toenail." His grin was unpleasant. Where was my beloved Daddy, always so good to me and so gentle?

"Be quiet, Jacob. You are making a fool of yourself--as usual."

Mama took up the battle, her back curved over the sink, her words sent like bullets to her favorite adversary. I resigned myself to my accustomed role of referee.

"You'd run back to her, wouldn't you? Just like that time when she was in the hospital and you were alone in the house with her husband. It's been so many husbands ago that I've forgotten his name. But," here he paused, and I heard again the pain and anger of that now ancient argument, "you left, and I always wondered what went on in that house between the two of you."

Mama dropped a plate into the sink, and the sound of the shattering pieces matched the sharp intake of her breath. Time hung in the breathless stillness. She turned around, and I could not believe the look of hatred that turned her face into an aged goddess of war. "You disgust me! How dare you even suggest that I would do anything like that with my poor sister in the hospital! Unless you apologize, I will never speak to you again."

And there went the plans for the big party. Foolish old people....

Mama, unyielding in her blind sense of family duty, and Daddy, out to pull his sister-in-law down from her pedestal where the little girl Marsha had placed her beloved older sister so many years ago.

"Please, Mama," I said. She waved me away. "Please, Daddy," I begged, grasping his hand like the favored child I had been.

I could not reach either one. They deflected my pleas as if they were just some annoying insects.

"She has to speak first," he said with weary stubbornness that was as weak as his body had become.

"Tell your mother I don't want any leftovers, " he complained to me.

"Tell your father that what's on his plate is what he gets."

In all honesty, Mama continued to perform her household duties, and Daddy received nutritious meals for his starving soul. The war finally ran out of bullets months later, but, as with most wars, hostilities continued to darken our private world. In his eyes, Daddy had evened the score, but I detected no light of victory there.

Life dealt Mama a brutal irony five years later. Daddy developed cancer and died within six awful weeks. Mama and he found each other again; loving and youthful once more, they clung together as she leaned over his hospital bed. "Eat, my darling. You need your strength. I will bring you some chicken soup tomorrow."
She did and fed him lovingly, wiping his emaciated face and begging us to let her sleep by his side.

I could hear Mama whispering, "Sweetheart, remember that pink dress you like so much? I'll wear it tomorrow when I visit you."

"You will always be my lovely, brown-haired darling." He tried to lift his hand to touch her face, but it fell weakly back to the sheet.

Mama bent over, kissed his hand, and rested her head on his chest. I stayed away, trying to cope with my own pain as well as theirs.

My father died quietly. My mother's cries shook the hospital walls. "Jacob! Jacob!" She wailed. "Are you really gone?"

He was indeed gone, and we discovered a week later that his deadliest enemy, Aunt Alice, had died on the same day. This was a war that had no winner.

Aunt Alice's Will

I saw Aunt Alice only once after her stroke, but the visit disturbed me. I hadn't seen my aunt for many years, but I didn't expect such dramatic changes.

What a shock. When we hugged and kissed, it was like holding a bundle of bones covered by cloth. Aunt Alice's right side was weakened, her speech slurred and difficult to hear. I asked the usual questions about her recovery, but my eyes took in her white hair with a few strands of brown looking like strangers among the snowy neighbors. Her skin, wrinkled and darkened by years of sun worshipping, hung in loose folds, but there was an anguished awareness in her dark brown eyes that hurt me.

"Yes, darling, I am not the aunt you remember. Your beautiful Aunt Alice who loved to dance at all the weddings and flirt with all the men." It was strange to hear her talk about herself as if she had separated from her vibrant and joyful younger self. She held one of my hands in her stronger hand, while the other one rested lifelessly on her leg. I compared the thin fingers distorted by arthritis with the graceful hand I remembered, fingernails painted a pale pink in order not to detract from her cherished diamond ring.

"Considering the fact that you've suffered a major health problem, I think you are doing remarkably well." Her friend Rita, who spent almost every day keeping Aunt Alice company, nodded and winked at my lies.

"Yes," Rita said, "Isn't she wonderful? She has a live-in aide, but insists on doing so much herself. She even makes her own breakfast and sends her aide out for a walk, like today. Such a good heart."

Aunt Alice visibly brightened, pulling herself up in her chair and letting go of my hand to pat her hair into place. It was the gesture of a once beautiful woman. "Thank God I can still...." She groped for a word causing Rita to move closer and whisper in her ear. "Thank God I can still live in my own apartment. I love it here." She waved her hand vaguely toward the window. Stretching my neck, I could see a portion of the beach and a bit of the rolling waves from a gray ocean, reflecting the darkness of approaching evening.

"Can you still walk down to the beach? I noticed some nice benches facing the ocean." I directed my question more to Rita than to Aunt Alice, who had drifted off into her thoughts. Was she remembering the daily swims she used to take every morning? The family warned her that swimming in the cold ocean could be very foolish at her age.

"Nonsense," she always said, "It's good to be active at any age, and it keeps my muscles strong." I knew she was something of a health fanatic, using wheat germ and extra vitamins before health foods became so popular. It was hard to accept this querulous, sick woman as the aunt who had had more energy than any of her sisters. She interrupted my thoughts with, "You'd think that Goldie and Nettie would come to see me more often. I could die here and they wouldn't even know it."

What she said didn't surprise me. Aunt Alice had always demanded attention from her family. But Rita's head bobbing up and down in sympathy sent out danger signals. Unbidden came a question: Where is the diamond watch Aunt Alice always wore for company? "It will be yours someday," she told me. I watched Rita as she hovered around Aunt Alice like a tiny, angry bumble bee.

"Your aunts," Rita confided with a frown, "really neglect poor Alice. They come once in a blue moon and then stay a few short hours. It's a shame the way they neglect her." She fluttered about, straightening my aunt's sweater and patting her arms in a proprietary manner that annoyed me.

I found myself blurting out, "Well, Rita, my mother lives in California now, but she writes every week. Her hands shake, but she writes anyhow. And I try to keep in touch as well."

"Oh yes, I know that. Alice loves you and your mother. Too bad you live so far away." Guilt and anger collided in my thoughts. But then I smiled. I could hear Mama's voice, "Soon she will ask us to commute already."

I paused to allow my emotions to subside. What was there about Aunt Alice's apartment that made me so uncomfortable? Her small red and gold Oriental rugs stirred memories of her luxurious home before her divorce. Some of the chairs and tables came from her old home but looked out of place in these tiny rooms. I saw my son's picture on the pale ivory table behind Aunt Alice. Pain charged through my body. Did Aunt Alice remember that I had lost this innocent-eyed boy a few years ago? I longed for her to comfort me.

Rita took the picture from my hand, and, turning so my aunt couldn't see, put it back on the table. "Such a terrible loss. Please don't talk about it with Alice. She cried so much when your brother wrote. I try to protect her from sad news." Who was this stranger pushing herself between my aunt and me?

Anger rose again in my head, throbbing like a red light that warned of danger ahead. I made a huge effort to act calmly, if only to dissolve the tension in the room. I moved my chair closer to Aunt Alice, a child again in my determination to prove to Rita that I had been like a daughter to my aunt. I had not the slightest compunction about turning my back on Rita and saying,"I need your love more than ever, Aunt Alice."

I rejoiced to hear Aunt Alice say, "Sweetheart, my heart hurts for you. I remember him as a cute little boy running all over your mother's apartment." Tears trickled down into the deep lines of her face, but her eyes remained grayed over and distant. I held her in my arms and let her cry and cry. For a moment, I lost touch with my own tragedy--whose child were we mourning? I was comforting her because I knew she was sad and bewildered.

In a soft, little voice she said, "Poor Harry. He was too young to die." I sat up startled. She had retreated to her own memories of my uncle whom she had loved so much.

Rita frowned at me. She moved quickly to my Aunt's side, mouthing the words, "See what happened?" Aunt Alice sniffled as Rita tenderly rubbed her arms and covered her shoulders with a soft white shawl. It was clear that Aunt Alice no longer controlled her life; Rita had taken over. I left after an uncomfortable hour of sporadic conversation which failed to lift my aunt's spirits. Once in a while I caught a glimpse of that gamine smile that always endeared her to others, but for the most part, she sat quietly looking toward the ocean.

When I was about to leave, she cried on my shoulder. "Darling Carole, write to me more often. Tell my darling sister that I think of her every day and wish that God will be good to her." It was hard to leave knowing I would never see her again. Of that I was sure. When she died, a part of my past would go with her as well. She was the strongest tie to Mama's childhood in Horadisht.

The inevitable came a year later with a letter from Rita telling us of Aunt Alice's death. Mama, in terrible pain over Daddy's death, wept as she added Aunt Alice's picture to the family grouping near the now somewhat shabby chair that she had used in the Bronx to preside over holiday gatherings. "I will put flowers around my dear sister's picture. She will never die if we remember her." With that statement, she turned her head to stare at me, with such intensity that I knew I had received another one of Mama's commandments.

The next shock came in the form of anguished letters from Aunt Goldie and Aunt Nettie. "Alice's will leaves us a few hundred each, but most of her money goes to Rita. Such a crime, Marsha, she even gets all the furniture and jewelry." My mind flashed to the diamond watch. Mama must have read my guilty thoughts.

She surprised me. "It's not wrong, my daughter," she said, her face firm and her eyes pensive behind the old-fashioned glasses she insisted on keeping. "After all, it's Rita who was with her almost every day."

"But Mama," I protested, "Aunt Alice had a live-in aide who did all the cooking and cleaning as well as taking care of Aunt Alice. Rita visited and maybe made her a cup of tea." Something in me refused to accept Rita's triumph. Was she wearing the watch I had coveted all these years?

Mama raised one slim finger in regal disapproval, "Remember, it's not the food or the cleaning Aunt Alice wanted. It was the love she needed from her family." Her eyes pinned me to my chair. Once again the message was clear: I expect you to be with me when I need you.

I suspect that if Mama had been in New York she would have rallied the family. Perhaps with her determined backing, the lawyers might have tried harder. But alone, Aunt Goldie and her little shadow, Aunt Nettie, waged a helpless legal battle against the will. They were too old and naive to understand the court's decree that forbade them to enter their sister's house looking for family pictures or keepsakes. Aunt Goldie wrote, "What should we do, Marsha? Even our own lawyer tells us we have to obey the court and stay away from poor Alice's apartment. God should only punish that miserable Rita."

When she learned that even family treasures were off limits to them, Mama responded soothingly at first, but then she, too, broke down. "The pictures, the pictures," she raged. "Only Alice had a picture of Papa."

Something left Mama dry-eyed and listless. She no longer had the strength to fight as she had when Uncle Harry's will caused a split in the family. Rita was a faceless enemy who had the law on her side. Mama spoke through lips that were pressed together in the way my family recognized so well, "That woman turned my sister against her own family. My poor sick sister didn't know she had a witch for a friend." Mama no longer remembered Rita's kindness.

She could only sigh and pile more and more plastic flowers around the picture of laughing Aunt Alice whose body almost danced with energy, denying the reality of the shrine Mama had built for her.

Daddy's picture stood nearby. I thought I detected a mocking smile playing around his full, sensitive mouth. His eyes, cynical and knowing, said, "See, I told you Alice always won. Your poor Mama. My silly Marsha. Always a slave to her dream of a perfect family."

Daddy was right. Poor Mama. In losing the battle with Rita, Mama had lost a part of her childhood. Never again did I hear the story of how her lovely sister left for New York while the little girl Marsha made up sweet songs to fill her lonely hours.

Time erased the lonely, fragile Aunt Alice from my memory. Instead when I think of her now, her arms reach out impatiently as lively music invites us to dance. She holds me close and we move with the rhythms we both love, our heads close together, her hand resting lightly on my back. Sometimes she forgets and calls me Marsha.

1988 Mama Saw the Daffodils One More Time

"I can't go see her yet, Michael; it's too soon."

My brother shifted uncomfortably in his chair. He let his breath out in two noisy puffs, a habit he acquired after we had to place Mama in a nursing home. "Listen, Carole, she keeps asking for you. Every time I go, I get, 'So where's my daughter? Is she too busy to come to see me? It's been months.'"

I took the bait and protested, "Not months, just three weeks." Just? How could I say that about the three horrible weeks since my husband had died?

"Yeah, but she doesn't know time any more. She sits there all day and stares at the television set; she doesn't hear a word. Or she fiddles with her greeting cards, turning them over and over trying to remember who the people were that sent them to her. It's no life."

Before Jack's final illness and death, I had visited Mama in the nursing home three times a week, dreading every visit, pushing the clock forward so I could finally stand up and say, "I have to make dinner for Jack. He's not well."

She'd always grab my hand and plead, "Just five more minutes, darling, please. Stay a while and talk to me." Sometimes my stomach churned as I watched her stirring her food around and around, making patterns in the mounds of peas, limp chicken, and rice. "Look at this; do you think he'll like what I made for him?"

I looked at the mess and said, "I don't know, Mama. Most of the time Michael eats with Jack and me. He comes right to our house after he leaves you." I hated it when she said such strange things. It made her seem like the other sad people in the nursing home.

Mama's head came up quickly, and I saw a flash of anger pass over her face. "Don't lie to me. He goes to that woman's house, doesn't he?" There was no woman, but I didn't answer.

Michael told me she kept track of my visits through some strange system in her head, yet she never even knew what day it was. I put my hand on my brother's arm, and he placed his own hand on mine. Neither one of us had ever been very demonstrative with one another, but the family bond remained strong. "Don't push me--I'm living on the edge. Make another excuse for me. Tell her that Jack is...." I couldn't finish without losing my control. Michael understood for he nurtured me the way he had always nurtured Mama.

Mama had been in the nursing home for over a year, but he continued to visit her twice a day, bringing her soup, cookies, and anything that he thought would bring a smile to her face. But she resented the time he took chatting with the nurses.

When Michael left my house, I wandered from room to room, pausing to straighten a picture, and to pull off a brown leaf from my plants, so sadly neglected. I had to lie down and sleep to escape my memories.

But I couldn't sleep. I kept seeing Mama when she was young and strong, a queen in her own house. Her voice, soft and sweet, sang in my head as if she were there beside me. I needed her to be the Mama who told me stories when I was ill, or even the Mama who came late to all my school events, but always came. Tomorrow I would go to see Mama. Finally I slept.

The next day I cleaned house with concentrated energy, as if the house were my enemy. She'll know about Jack, I thought. I can't lie to her. As I dusted and swept with mechanical efficiency, I repeated aloud, "Okay, Okay, I'll be there soon." Though it was only February, there was a hint in the air that heralded an early spring. From my bedroom, I could see the blossoms on the flowering peach tree fluttering and dancing to some inner music. The prospect of spring, even this artificial one, made me smile for the first time in three weeks. But sorrow washed over me once more. Human beings weren't like trees. Winter carries the sadness of endings.

I whispered softly, "Those white clouds will turn dark in a few days and the wind and rain will blow all those blossoms to the ground, like snow drifting down. How foolish to pretend that winter is over." When I had dusted and mopped everything, I still felt the need to keep moving. The house provided tomb-like silence for I had no desire to hear human voices nor even beautiful music. I glanced at the clock. "Yes, yes, I am coming," I said aloud, knowing that Mama sat alone and could watch the clock from her wheelchair.

I rushed around my kitchen, a packaged cake mix in my hand. Grimly precise, I emptied the mix into a bowl, added water and two eggs that stared back at me with watery yellow eyes after I dumped them into the bowl. I stirred, beat, and poured. Forty-five minutes later, I wrapped the hot cake in a dishtowel and headed for my desperate visit, determined to protect Mama from the sad news.

When I pulled my car up to the entry of the nursing home, I sat still and held the warm cake against my leg. Inside the halls echoed with high-pitched voices and sounds of carts being rolled along the shiny tile floors.

At Mama's door, I stopped to breathe deeply and walked in. Mama's roommate, who could no longer speak, must have heard from Michael about Jack's death. Her long, frail fingers went to her heart, and her eyes, warm and expressive, bathed me in loving-kindness. I nodded, afraid to say anything that would open the floodgates.

Mama's aide, a sweet Hispanic woman, finished wiping the food that trailed from my mother's mouth. Mama had left behind all the years of absolute independence and neatness. "Clean your plate," she'd say or "Pick up your room before dinner." Here she was playing like a child with her dinner, most of it remaining on her tray. Her fingers, orange with smashed carrot bits, wandered to her hair, leaving behind colored droppings like strange flowers in the long, snow-white strands.

A pang of sorrow shot through me as Mama turned, caught sight of me, stretched out her arms, and asked, "Is it really you, my daughter? Have you come to see me? It's been at least a year."

I allowed her to hug and kiss me, though I knew I'd have to pick the orange flecks out of my clothing afterward. "Don't be silly, Mama. It's only been a few weeks." To calm myself, I showed Mama the fresh-baked cake which she immediately dug into with those child-like fingers.

"Wait, wait, Mama, we'll find a fork and a plate." I blessed the flurry of activity that brought a pale pink blush to her still soft cheeks and a peal of laughter to her lips.

"A party, a party. Is it my birthday?" She looked at me, her eyes momentarily puzzled by a memory that refused to do her bidding.

"No, darling. Your birthday was last month, remember? January 9th." I hurt. Only five days before the 9th, Jack and I had celebrated his birthday with a cake much like the one I baked for Mama. I was glad she didn't remember the two birthdays.

Mama turned her head, and looked out the large window at the bare trees. "I hate the winter days," she said, her voice sounded like she was talking to herself, "I want to see flowers and little children playing." Suddenly, she turned back to face me. "Make the winter go away, my darling daughter."

I knelt by her wheelchair and laid my head in her lap. "When I was a little girl, you told me that every spring flowers would bloom on your Papa's grave because you had spread flower seeds all over the earth. I want to see the flowers too, Mama. I'm so cold inside."

Her arms around me tightened their grip. She lifted my head up and said, "What has happened to you, dear child? Why are you so sad?"

For a moment, I struggled to remain silent, as I had promised my brother I would. But overwhelmed by a desire to be a child again in my mother's arms, I let the tears roll down and sobbed in ragged abandon. The hospital corridors were silent. No one responded quickly to human outbursts except to wipe up afterward. Mama and I remained locked in lonely embrace.

"He's gone, Mama. Jack is gone." Mama cried too, but she was rocking me back and forth in those wonderful Mama arms, murmuring nonsense syllables that I remembered from childhood.

I rested against her as she sang some sweet song in Yiddish. I didn't understand the words, but I knew she was comforting me, though her voice was cracked like a piece of delicate crystal that had once been perfect and strong. It no longer mattered that her hair was straight and stringy, nor that her fingers still had bits of carrots on the tips. Mama came back to me when I needed her the most.

She lasted until April and enjoyed the daffodils one more time. With Mama gone, I will never be a little girl again.

1990 Aunt Goldie's Birthday

Aunt Goldie celebrated her 87th birthday in June. She looked every year of her age, just as Mama did when she had died five years before at 92. Three years before Mama died, Aunt Goldie came to see her. They cried, shouted into each other's ears, and said goodbye while sorrow, struggling like a wounded bird beating its wings, whispered, "I'll never see you again, my sister." Mama said afterwards, "What happened to my baby sister? She got so old."

Mama would have been even more upset if she had seen Aunt Goldie at her party, thin gray hair hanging straight from an all-too visible scalp, her gait halting and stiff as she pushed her walker to where I sat. I spoke to her as she tried to get comfortable in the straight-backed chair her daughter set out for her.

She peered at me without any understanding. "What did you say, darling Carole? I have so much trouble with my hearing. It's hot here in Stella's house. Pretty soon I think Dad and I should go home." I hesitated, not knowing whether to repeat my insincere compliment about the "pretty green blouse" that fit her shrunken shoulders so badly. Instead, I decided to just pat her mottled hand, seeing with the eyes of memory her lovely long fingers.

"I brought you pictures of my grandbaby, Aunt Goldie."

She nodded her head at my answer. "He is adorable, but he doesn't look like anyone in our family. It's too bad your mother didn't live to have pleasure from him. It's good to see you smile. You had enough trouble in your life. It's time for joy." It was hard to be joyful when I saw what Aunt Goldie looked like. So many years had passed.

Mama always scolded Aunt Goldie for talking about growing old. "Nonsense, Goldie. You're a beautiful young woman yet. What's a few gray hairs? With you, your hair will always be red. But darling, don't you think it's a little too red?"

Time grabbed Mama along with the other aunts and uncles who are gone. I'm like Aunt Goldie; I don't want to think about the others.

Aunt Goldie peered at me, "You only look like your mother when you smile. Funny how we sisters all ended up looking like Bubbie as we got so old."

I asked Aunt Goldie if she remembered anything about her childhood. She laughed and said, "Russia? What nonsense. Who wants to think of those years?"

She pulled at her hearing aid and complained, "Why can't you young people speak clearly. Everyone asks me questions, so many questions." For a minute, I thought she was falling asleep, but she said, "Everything sounds like babble. If Dad wouldn't get upset, I'd pull this silly thing out."

It was obvious that Aunt Goldie couldn't follow much of what I wanted to ask her. When she was in the mood to talk about the past, perhaps she would.

She fingered the pearl buttons on her blouse and said, " Dad and I should have stayed in Florida. But I should be grateful. My daughter has a beautiful big home. Who ever heard of a living room with red walls? Her coffee table is big enough for ten people to sit on. All the soft furniture is not for me, but did you see her movie star bathroom?"

"Aunt Goldie, do you remember this picture?" I placed it in her hands so she could bring it up close to her eyes.

"Yes, darling. That's your mother and your Aunt Nettie. You thought old ladies lose their memory of their own sisters? Of course I remember. Everyone shows me pictures of years ago. Who wants to be reminded of the days when I could hear everything everyone said, I could eat what I wanted to eat, take a bus to go shopping and talk to my sisters for an hour on the telephone? Vey is meir, what the years have done!"

Then she smiled and pointed to my brother, who smiled back at her from across the room.

"Michael is such a lovely boy. What am I saying? His hair is as white as mine. Even the children are getting older. Who knew that this could happen? Just look at this picture, your mother and I and Nettie were all dressed up for a big charity dinner at a fancy restaurant in New York. The three of us went to Macys a week before and schlepped dresses from the racks for a whole afternoon. We finally found the dresses you see in this picture." I kept very still. I had never heard her speak like this.

She ran her arthritic fingers over the picture and whispered to herself, "Look at my hair. At least thirty years ago. Dad remembers when it was more red than gold. He loved to touch it whenever we kissed. When was the last time we kissed? Old people don't kiss. We were young once--all of us squeezed in happily in the big house in Brooklyn." Aunt Goldie looked at Uncle Seymore, then wrapped herself up in her memories, her eyes seeing what I couldn't see, her ears having no problems with the voices of her youth....

Goldie watched Alice primping in front of her dresser mirror. She's so beautiful. I wished I looked like her. "Alice, who are you going out with tonight?"

"Just some man I met at a dance for garment workers. It was so romantic. It turned out that he was my boss. Just the kind of man I've been waiting for. Handsome, a good dancer--and rich."

Goldie smiled and said, "Rich? That's not important. Do you love him?" Goldie was just 18 and beginning to dream about a special man she could marry and love forever.

Alice rouged her round cheeks that even her brothers liked to pinch. Her fingers carefully fluffed out her short, dark curls while she examined her face from all angles. She bounced to her feet, turning to check that her new polka dot dress looked just as pretty from the rear as it did in the mirror. Then she took a flower from a vase, put it into her mouth between her teeth and pretended to be a vamp. She laughed at the astonishment on Goldie's face, kissed her, and waved as she ran lightly down the steps in front of the big, brown house. She took the hand of the young man who waited for her.

Nettie joined Goldie at the window, pushing aside the crisp white curtains so they could watch Alice as she

walked, leaning close to her date and talking animatedly.
"My Marvin took me out last night," Nettie said. We went
by bus to Coney Island, strolled on the boardwalk, had an
ice-cream cone and came home."

"That sounds like a nice date. Why do you look so
annoyed?"

"He didn't even kiss me goodnight."

Goldie comforted her older sister. "Next time, give
him a little help. Pucker up your lips like this." Nettie
looked shocked, but she listened to Goldie, who was
already very popular with the boys at the factory.
Everyone admired her shiny red hair and her happy smile.

The next morning, the sisters and brothers rushed
around competing for the bathroom and then finding time
for a quick breakfast before they left for work. It was a
warm morning, and the girls worried that their hair, which
they had tried to curl with papers, would look terrible
before they even had time to hurry to the subway.

Her mama scolded Goldie for leaving her clothes
on the bathroom floor. "I am not your maid. Don't act
like a fine lady. It's enough that Alice gives herself airs."
Goldie dashed back to pick up her clothes.

Marsha slipped into one of the ladder-backed chairs
around the long table in the kitchen that bore the marks of
hot plates and careless scratches from forks and knives.
She helped herself to a bowl of hot oatmeal and said, "If
Alice acts like a fine lady, it's because she is one. She
already has a good job, and her boss is in love with her."

Goldie smiled as she joined the family. Alice had
just met her boss at a dance, so how could they talk about
love so soon? Besides she knew that Alice could do no
wrong in Marsha's eyes. How often she had to listen to
Marsha's stories about the pretty straw hat that Alice had
given her before she had left for America to look for work.

Nettie came over and whispered in Goldie's ear,
"Pretty soon Marsha will take that silly hat out and show us

how she danced with it." Goldie put her hand in front of her mouth so Marsha wouldn't see her laughing.

Goldie helped herself to another glass of milk from the big blue pitcher in the middle of the table. Although she was younger than Nettie, she loved her best. Nettie was shy and turned to Goldie for advice or comfort when she was upset. After helping Mama with the dishes, Goldie said to Nettie, "Let's hurry to the bus stop. Marvin promised he'd introduce me to his best friend Seymore. Our older sisters plan to marry soon." Her face was wistful. "You have Marvin. It's time for me to find a boyfriend, too."

Nettie put her arm around Goldie. "You're still so young. Just have fun meeting a lot of different boys. Look at some of the married women in our dress shop. They come in tired every morning, complaining that they have to work as well as cook and clean their houses."

Marsha followed the two sisters as they skipped down the porch steps. She called after them, "Don't forget to pick up some fruit on your way home. I have a ...friend coming for dinner." She smiled and blushed.

Goldie stopped in her rush, turned to Marsha, and said, "You have a man friend coming to dinner?"

Marsha smoothed her hair and tugged at her black skirt before she answered. "He's nice. His name is Jacob and he goes to college at night."

Nettie, too, came back to the steps and said, "College? Wonderful, Marsha. I hope he has his feet on the ground. You're such a dreamer." Marsha waved her hand in dismissal and hurried back into the house. Goldie tugged at Nettie's arm. "Let's walk faster. See, even our quiet Marsha has found a boyfriend."

When she and Nettie arrived at the trolley stop, they saw Marvin and another young man. As they came closer, Goldie couldn't stop staring at Marvin's friend. "What shiny black hair! And see, he has a mustache. Just like the actors in the movies."

All the way from Brooklyn to 7th Avenue in Manhattan where they both worked, Goldie and Seymore sat side by side on the trolley. "Pretty soon," Seymore confided, "I'm going to get out of this rat race in the clothing trade and be my own boss." Even though he talked rapidly about his plans, his eyes went to Goldie's hair, red-gold in the morning sun.

She nodded her head in appreciation. "I think that's wonderful. I don't know anyone who owns his own business. What will you do?"

Seymore straightened his jacket, wiped some dust from his shoes, and said firmly, "My brother and I have saved some money and want to buy a truck. My father was a painter in the old country and he will teach us the European way to paint houses. We don't want to be stuck in a shop cutting pants all our lives." Whenever the trolley lurched forward, Seymore moved closer to Goldie, holding her arm so she wouldn't fall. She wished the ride to Manhattan would never end.

That night the table had to accommodate four young men, all dressed in neat, dark suits, despite the heat. They ate baked chicken and roasted potatoes, taking time to compliment their hostess, who kept bringing out more platters of vegetables and coleslaw from the warm kitchen. Goldie could hardly sit still. I have a new friend, she thought. Maybe he'll like me enough to be my boyfriend. She sighed, then realized everyone was looking at her, including Seymore. She fanned her face with one of Mama's big linen napkins and said, "It's just very warm in here. I mean there are so many people tonight. Oh, gosh, I don't know what I mean." Nettie pinched her leg under the table.

When her face no longer sent out signals of her emotions, Goldie let her eyes wander back to Seymore who was trying to answer her brothers' questions. The oldest brothers took over the job of sizing up the men and their futures. "What do you get paid in the garment factory?" was a favorite question. They were impressed with Seymore's plans to go out on his own.

Goldie had time to stare at Seymore and notice again his stylish, thin mustache. Tomorrow he's taking me to Coney Island. I hope we go up on the Ferris wheel. It terrifies me to look out over the ocean from way up there. But I can always tell Seymore to hold me around. Maybe he'll kiss me. Wonder what a mustache feels like. Her face burned again, but she smiled because no one was watching her. Seymore talked with confidence that certainly seemed to impress her brothers. She sighed a different kind of sigh. Life was so perfect at this moment. If only she could put a magic spell on the clock. It was so nice to be young.

Mama bustled about the table in the dining room, rearranging the plates as she added fruits and nuts while Nettie and Marsha helped her to clear the table, laughing and flirting with their own young men. The dining room was Goldie's favorite room. She loved the square, fringed chandelier which cast a golden glow over the oak table as the family sat around and talked happily. Mama kept her most precious dishes in the wide sideboard; nobody except Mama put the dishes away after dinner.

I'm grownup, Goldie told herself. How lovely to be part of a family like mine, everyone loving everyone else. Tonight I'll ask Alice how to put rouge on my cheeks.

Aunt Goldie looked confused when my cousin Stella interrupted her memories. Uncle Seymore was yawning and stretching his legs.

"Mother, you look so tired. All this partying may be too much for you, even on your birthday."

Goldie kissed Stella gratefully and replied, "Such a mitzvah. I heard every word you said. Thank God for all miracles. Come, Dad, Stella is right. I am tired. Michael offered to take us home."

I felt the tears rising in my eyes when Aunt Goldie held me for a long time. She just looked into my eyes, and I envisioned Mama smiling at both of us. Aunt Goldie wiped her eyes and said, " I can't wait to climb into bed. Dad will give me the medicine the doctor ordered and help me into my nightgown. He is a dear, good husband. Tomorrow I will make him a baked apple with raisins, his favorite dessert."

I saw her touching Uncle Seymore's arm. He smiled down at her and my mind flashed to Mama's stories of the young Goldie with the lovely red hair falling in love with a quietly confident Uncle Seymore. Now she said, "As long as I can see Dad next to me in the bed, I can rest easy." I could tell that it was too much noise and excitement tonight for an old lady. Eighty-seven today. The only one left of her whole family of brothers and sisters. I thought of Mama's long years without Daddy. Aunt Goldie was lucky to have Uncle Seymore by her side.

I imagined them holding hands after turning off the lights. "Good night, Dad," she'd say.

"Good night, dear. Happy birthday."

1991   The Next Generation Feud

It was noisy and warm in the Chinese restaurant where all my Southern California cousins gathered for the surprise birthday party Stella's husband had planned for her. I turned to Judy, a few years older than I and sighed.

"How can our little cousin be fifty years old?" I asked Judy. "Beats me," my cousin answered. "We just don't see each other often enough. I'd like to organize a cousins' reunion every year. We aren't getting any younger."

As Judy looked around, her face lit up at the excited group, which included her cute grandsons who tried to act grown-up but tugged away at their party clothes in obvious discomfort. Everywhere the bright red, green, and gold wallpaper zapped us with color and excitement. While the girls fixed each other's hair, the boys shifted from foot to foot and groaned, "When do we eat?"

"Now remember," their grandmother said to them and the other children, "everyone shouts 'Surprise' when Stella walks in." The children nodded solemnly but then squealed when they heard the waiters' footsteps near the door of the banquet room.

Our host tried to control the hubbub. He rolled his eyes at Judy, who nodded and went from child to child with whispered instructions. Amazingly, they all calmed down.

When the guest of honor finally strolled in the door, she stopped in shock as shouts of 'surprise' filled the room, then she burst into tears.

"Oh, my God, my brother is here from Texas and Carole and Michael from up north! How wonderful!" Stella went from guest to guest, embracing, hugging, and exclaiming, "What a great surprise!" When she reached Judy, she stopped, shrugged, and kissed her quickly on the cheek.

Now what's that about, I wondered. Stella looked flushed and upset, yet tried to smile when she chose a chair next to me. She squeezed my hand then leaned over to help a frustrated little one whose napkin kept sliding off her lap. A waiter passed me with a large tureen. I could almost taste the sweet and sour soup, so pungent was the aroma as he ladled some for each guest at our table. My stomach growled in anticipation.

Stella said to me, "I can't believe Judy would come." She twisted her napkin in her hand, glaring at her husband, who avoided her eyes. "The nerve of her. I told her I didn't want to speak to her again."

I put my arm around Stella to calm her down. "Tell me what's happened. Relax. This is *your* party and we're all here to celebrate and love you."

"Love me? You've got to be kidding! I'll kill my husband for inviting her. He knew we had a terrible argument."

"He was smart to try to smooth it over. What did you argue about that could be this bad? You and Judy have been so close ever since you moved to California." I knew there had been some problems, but I decided not to say anything.

"Close is one thing. Suffocated is something else."

Judy watched us from across the room, her warm hazel eyes heavy with emotion. Between courses, I walked around to her table and pulled a chair over next to hers. When I began to speak, Judy lifted her hand and said, "Carole, you don't know anything. Stella's been feeding your ears with nonsense. I really think she's finally blown her top."

I swallowed hard, thought of Mama's injunction, "Family is everything." and spoke with a shivery feeling in my gut. "Listen, nothing is so bad that communication won't make it better. Stella cares about you, but her nerves are so frayed from working hard that she blasts off at anyone who tries to tell her to slow down."

"She must slow down. I offered to help out while she and Jay take a vacation. She almost bit my head off. They are killing themselves."

"Killing ourselves!" I jumped. Stella stood behind my chair, her words cutting through the air like the circus magician's swift swords. "What I do is my business. I've listened to your advice for so many years, choking on it just because I'm the kid cousin. Let me breathe, for God's sake!" Her face whitened as she spoke.

Judy stood up and moved closer to Stella. "Calm down. This is exactly what I meant. You're so burned out you can't accept love when it's offered to you."

She put her hand on Stella's arm who pushed it away in an angry gesture that shocked everyone into silence. Through clenched teeth, she said, "I am no longer playing your game. Over and over you keep telling me how to run my life. You're not my mother. Stop trying to control me."

Even the children sat with frightened faces, not understanding the angry voices around them. Judy and Stella stood with tight faces, bodies tense.

The air in my throat almost strangled me. I had a quick memory of Mama and Judy facing each other across a table in the Bronx so long ago. The same kind of anger, that time about money, this time about control. I clasped my hands in a praying gesture and said, "Please, please. Not again, not again."

Judy turned, stared at me as if she hadn't heard a word, marched stiffly to a plant she had left in the corner and plunked it down in front of Stella. "This is not meant to be your birthday gift. It was my way of telling you that families are alive, too, and need nurturing to be healthy." Judy signaled to her husband to follow and, without another word, walked out. Judy's daughters conferred in whispers, then went over to Stella. One said, "It's best for us to leave; Mom needs us now. It's really a shame...." Her words drifted off into nothingness, as she raised her shoulders in frustration, gathered her children, and left.

The headwaiter nodded happily at all the commotion, perhaps thinking it was part of the celebration. He picked up the dirty dishes, refreshed the water in our glasses, then set out steaming bowls of rice and vegetables, shiny with oil and succulent sauces. I watched him as he moved around our table explaining the contents of each platter to guests who had little desire to continue eating.

The older daughter lingered, then put her arms around Stella with a rueful, "Happy Birthday. Sorry, kiddo." She too left.

Stella sat down heavily, and played with her food, her chopsticks making aimless circles around the plate. My heart went out to her, but I decided she didn't want any more cousinly advice. By now, the party had disintegrated so badly that the remaining guests ate in total silence.

I slipped into the chair next to Judy's sister, Sarah. "Do you think Judy will come back when she sees that so many people left?" I asked.

"Are you kidding? This argument has been brewing for a long time, but we all hoped they would avoid an open break. I guess I should leave, too, or Judy will feel bad."

I banged my hand on the table, hard enough to make the silverware dance around crazily. "I don't understand why two grown-ups can't discuss their differences. We're family, not strangers." I wondered how Mama and Aunt Goldie would have acted. I supposed I didn't learn to be as good at Mama in a family crisis.

Sarah's bitter laugh startled me, "Do you know how much you sounded like your mother just now? What did being family do to the argument over Uncle Harry's will--except make it worse?" I had no ready answer. I felt Mama's sorrowful presence all around us. Michael looked at me and ruefully smiled. I knew he wouldn't get involved.

About a year later, Judy joined us in Northern California for a visit. We relaxed on her daughter's deck in Berkeley, lazily enjoying the spring sunshine. When the conversation turned to family matters, I was shocked to hear that she and Stella had not spoken to each other in all that time. "Why didn't anyone tell me what was happening?" I said.

"Your life has been difficult enough since you've been alone. We tried to keep all family stresses from you. When we saw you at the party, we were shocked to see what grieving had done to you."

Her answer quieted me, for I had turned inward since I had lost Jack. Yet something of Mama must have been passed on to me, for I experienced real pain at the thought of this new feud. I tried reasoning as I had done last year, "Both of you are educated women. You are too mature to allow small differences to explode into nasty arguments."

Judy set her lips in a manner that immediately brought Mama's angry expression vividly back to life. "She owes me an apology. When we tried to call them the next day, they were both so rude that I decided I would never bother calling again."

"Never is a terrible word. Aunt Goldie moved to California to be near Stella. How are you going to see her without bumping into Stella?"

Judy's face twisted for a moment. I could see that I had touched a sensitive spot. "Aunt Goldie means a great deal to me, and I'll try not to let her know. She's the only aunt left."

Judy and I stared at each other, and I knew she remembered the anguish of the old feud.

She smiled wanly and said, "Maybe it's in the blood."

I shuddered at her words and grimly set myself up as the arbitrator. I could not accept the fact that I had inherited Mama's blind loyalty. On the telephone and in letters, I tried to explain each opposing point of view first to Judy, then to Stella. "Judy said she hated to see you work so hard. She offered to help many times."

Stella's quiet voice wiped out my hope, "No one can take over my life. I'm tired of advice that simply hides her poor opinion of me."

I pleaded with Judy, "Listen, you are more experienced. Swallow some pride and make an attempt to get back together." She wrote, "Everything you told me makes me even more sure that they are wrong."

My brother consoled me, "Stop knocking yourself out. You are simply making things worse. What difference does their silly argument make to you?"

Even so, I tried to act as a subtle go-between, especially when Judy's husband developed serious health problems. "Isn't it awful?" I asked Stella when I called with the news. She agreed quietly but offered nothing more.

"The holidays are coming," I said to Judy when she called. "Will you visit Aunt Goldie?"

"Of course, Carole. We don't neglect her."

Much remains unspoken, but I hear the regret and the pain. Mama's Papa once told her that sometimes families are the last to change. Though they still love each other, pride hardens their hearts. He was as wise as Mama had said.

I'm tired of being the go-between. Whatever it takes to change this sad impasse must come from Stella and Judy. I am content to love them both, for powerful family ties surface to remind us of the past, even as we move away year by year from our parents' time. We stay in touch, no longer in the noisy family gatherings, but through letters and phone calls when we want to share our joys or our sorrows.

I have the feeling that we cousins will be the last to carry on the traditions and memories that Mama held to be so precious. Our children blend into a different lifestyle, and most of their thoughts are of the future. Family feuds are not likely to be part of their lives, and for that I am grateful.

It embarrasses me to admit that a second cousin, Uncle Saul's granddaughter, no longer wants to speak to me. For a year she and I developed a long distance friendship. It exploded into nothingness when we had a disagreement, a foolish one. However, since she was relatively new in my life, I accepted her desire to cut off our correspondence. I wish her well, but I have no room for family feuding.

Judy and Stella have met at sad events and were civil to one another. I see them both but stay out of that part of their lives. We love in different ways.

LAST WORDS

1999 Epilogue

Spring moves quickly into summer and my house is calm, despite the summer heat. My birthday passed with cards and flowers from my son and family. No more big hurrahs for me. I had my share and more in the past. My brother, his wife, my husband, and I celebrated quietly in elegant surroundings. Dessert came with candles that I obediently blew out and made my silent wish: please God, no more surprises for me. Life has been sweet these past few years, and I don't ask for anything else.

How different it all was from the days when Mama tried to surprise me. No feigned excitement, no pile of gifts--and no Mama. Yet it's still impossible to have a family celebration without feeling her presence at the table. I can see her now, raising her eyes at my brother's wife. "All right," I can hear her say in dry acceptance, "but better she should be Jewish. He looks happy." I don't know what she would say about my husband of three years, but I hope she would say something like, "I'm happy for you, my daughter. You have had enough pain. He looks like a good man. Wavy hair and a nice smile. A little like my Papa, so kind and caring."

My son, Ron, has his own life. Mama died before I lost our second son. For her sake, I'm happy she was spared that pain. Mama and Jack both missed the joy of our darling Jeremy, so far my only grandchild. He is my link to the future. My stories are for him.

All of Mama's sisters are gone now, Aunt Goldie last of all. While she lived, I could count on her love and memories. She had an uncanny resemblance to Mama or maybe very old ladies all look alike to me.

It doesn't help to hold on to the warped emotions of the past. Living in the eye of Mama's personal hurricane prepared me to be alone for almost ten years, to know myself, and to cherish the beauty of our close family ties.

Recently Michael offered me some of Mama's old furniture. "I'll take the tall dresser," I told him, knowing that I could fill it again with all the fascinating treasures that my imagination could dredge up. Memory will place the charming pink enamel watch back in the tiny pink box with the pink cotton, and tuck the little bits of ermine from my baby bonnet next to Mama's romantic postcards from Daddy when he was courting her. I also treasure the little books of poetry she pored over in her few quiet moments.

Nowhere could I find the faded little brown purse that Mama hid because it contained all the secret instructions that Uncle Harry had given her about his will. The demons that purse unleashed upon the family are mainly forgotten and rightly so.

The years have smoothed out and flattened the bumps and wrinkles of the cloth that bound the family together. The days when chaotic family relationships ruled our lives are gone with the aunts and uncles who lived so large in Mama's life. But Mama's stories told to me as a dreamy, romantic little girl remain as bright as the golden samovar she had to leave behind when Bubbie took her family to the new world of America.

While I pass on these stories to my son and grandson, I know I have written them to please Mama, to be once more the child who wanted only her approving smile and her words, "I am proud of you, my daughter. God will reward you with many years of happiness. My Papa told me that some day I would have a beautiful daughter, and he was right." I wish I could have Mama's steadfast faith in the power of goodness. But I feel grateful that I can see her smile and almost hear her voice. It took me almost a lifetime to realize she wanted the best for me, and that she truly believed that I could achieve whatever my heart desired.

Inspirational Notes

Inspirational Notes